STUCK ON FIRST

STUCK ON FIRST

EMILY FRENCH

To baseball lovers and romantics everywhere.

Love is the most important thing in the world, but baseball is pretty good, too.

— YOGI BERRA

How can you not be romantic about baseball?

— MONEYBALL

A hot dog at a game beats roast beef at the Ritz

— HUMPHREY BOGART

CHAPTER ONE

FIVE TOOL PLAYER - *A position player who has great skill in all the tools or basic skills: hitting for average, hitting for power, base running and speed, throwing, and fielding.*

"Oh my God, would you take a look at him. Come to Momma."

Hailey pulled her attention away from her score sheet. Her friend Molly had a pair of binoculars glued tighter to her face than a magnet on a refrigerator. Hailey could see that they were trained on the visiting dugout. Molly's long chestnut hair was piled up in a messy bun.

"Men are not meat, Molls," Hailey said as she returned her attention to the score sheet in her lap.

"Sure they are. That's why they're called beefcake," Molly snorted.

"Hot dogs...get your hot dogs. 100% all beef franks," a deep voice barked, ringing through the stadium.

"Here! Over here." Molly began waiving her arms wildly at the vendor. She turned to Hailey. "Speaking of beefcake. Want one?"

Hailey let out a big sigh. "Sure. Mustard and lots of napkins, please." She tucked a blond stray hair back behind her ear and re-adjusted her Dodgers cap. She carefully set her score sheet and program to one side of her lap as she took the hot dog from Molly's hands. She closed her eyes as she bit into it. A small groan escaped her lips, it tasted like baseball and memories. She opened her eyes as she chewed. The March sky in Arizona was a bright cornflower blue and warm, the sun was high above the desert. When she and Molly had left Los Angeles, it had been unusually cloudy and cold. The warmth was a welcome sensation. In Hailey's opinion there was nothing better than a spring training baseball game. The majestic Saguaro cactus and dramatic mountain ridges made up the Sonoran Desert surrounding the baseball stadium. The season was still full of hope and possibilities.

The air was filled with the familiar sounds of baseball: the crack of the bat, a booming voice over the PA, and the cheers of the fans. The smell of hot dogs and cotton candy mixed with the scent of freshly mown grass added to her sensory overload. Just then she caught a splash of bright yellow out of the corner of her eye.

"Oh my God, Molls! Look at my score sheet!" Hailey cried. A blob of mustard from her friend's hot dog had dripped out and now colored the top of the page. "It's covering the list of pitchers," Hailey lamented as she attempted to clean it off with a napkin. A bright yellow stain was left behind.

"I don't know why you do that anyways...there's a huge scoreboard right there." Molly pointed to the Jumbotron in right field with her elbow as she continued to eat.

"This is an official score keeping, including strikes and balls and how each out or run occurs. It's a tradition for me," Hailey said quietly. She felt a swell of emotion as she recalled attending Dodgers games with her grandpa who had taught her the art of score keeping. Her heart squeezed just a bit at the memory. Her small self in a blue Dodgers cap, her grandpa wearing his signature straw brimmed hat and Ray-Ban classic sunglasses on his face; he was the epitome of 1950s cool regardless of the decade. He had taught her the corresponding number to each defensive position and how to record each ball and strike on her score sheet. He had been a bright spot in a dark childhood.

"I'm sorry...I'll try to keep my mustard contained in the future." Molly gave her a smile and nudged Hailey with her shoulder.

It was part of why Hailey loved her as her friend. Most people only saw the overly confident, very driven, often sarcastic woman in Molly, but Hailey knew she also had a soft side. They had met in grade school and had been good friends ever since.

"It's no biggie, I'll live." Hailey smiled back at her friend.

They sat in silence for a bit, Hailey watching the game, Molly checking out the players.

"I think I'm going to swear off men." Hailey bit her lip as she focused on her score card.

Molly snorted. "Yeah, right. Right after California falls into the ocean. Remind me again what happened to the last guy." She set the binoculars down and leveled her gaze at Hailey.

"Same thing that always happens...a big fat nothing. A few dates and then poof...either they ghost me, or I ghost them." She shrugged her shoulders. She had a long history of failed relationships...if you could even call them relationships. They seldom made it past the first few dates. Her therapist said she was unknowingly sabotaging herself either by picking the wrong guys or by subconsciously dooming the relationship before it could even start. Dr.

Boone suggested that due to Hailey's childhood, she probably felt she didn't deserve to be loved or that she was even lovable. Seeking out affirmations, usually from men, was Hailey's way of trying to fill a void in her psyche. A void left by her parents. "This leads to a circle of failed relationships," Dr. Boone went on to explain. Hailey's need to feel loved pulled men, often the wrong kind, into her orbit. And when it was the "right" kind of guy, Hailey would push them away feeling she wasn't deserving of their love. A vicious cycle Hailey wasn't even aware was going on. She wasn't convinced this *was* what was occurring, but there was a small voice telling her that there could be *some* truth to it.

Her therapist had gone on to suggest that Hailey should take a break from dating to work on her self-confidence so she would choose a relationship for the right reasons and not to fill a hole left from her childhood. She let out another big sigh and spent several more minutes losing herself in the Zen-like feeling baseball gave her.

She felt her phone buzz in her pocket. She pulled it out and saw a photo of her dog looking happy on her screen. She immediately broke into a smile.

Molly leaned over. "Is that from Rob?"

"Yeah, he's watching Sandy for me." Sandy was Hailey's four-year-old dachshund named after Sandy Koufax, the greatest pitcher in baseball history in Hailey's opinion, although Rob was under the misguided delusion that it was Randy Johnson. She couldn't count the hours they had spent debating the subject.

"It's really nice that he watches Sandy for you. Have you ever considered…you know…hooking up with him?"

Hailey snorted in reply. "We're just friends…that's it…so no, I haven't considered 'hooking up' with him anymore than I've considered hooking up with you."

"Hey...I'm offended by that." Molly recoiled, a hand to her chest, pretending to be hurt.

"Ha ha...very funny. But seriously...if Rob were interested in me, he would have made a move sometime over all the years we've been friends, which has been like five years already. Right?"

The "Rob" Molly was speaking of, was one Rob Steadman. They had met in college when he found her sobbing in a quiet corner of the library. Heartbroken over getting a text from the guy she had been seeing, telling her that he was seeing someone else. Hailey literally couldn't remember the guy's name anymore; but what she did remember was seeing Rob appear out of nowhere, asking if she was okay. When she could only answer by shaking her head "yes," and then "no," he gently guided her out of the library and over to the cafeteria, buying her cookies and hot chocolate while listening to her sob story.

And Hailey *had* thought about Rob as more than a friend on more than a few occasions. He was handsome in a quiet way, smart, funny, and loved baseball about as much as she did. She had been drawn to him immediately. He made her feel warm inside. She always felt a bit of a flutter in her stomach when she saw him and often had to remind herself that they were just friends.

She had always held off from expressing anything more. If he was interested in her as more than a friend, Hailey was certain he would have made a move at some point. But he hadn't. Which put him squarely in the "friends-only" zone. She certainly didn't want to risk their relationship by making some sort of stupid overture that would end with Rob awkwardly telling her that he saw her as only a friend and that was it. Nope...she didn't need that kind of rejection on top of making it weird between them.

"Heads up!" a deep voice shouted.

Hailey looked up just in time to see a foul ball headed straight for them. She instinctively grabbed her mitt and caught it before it smashed into Molly's head.

"Well that was close." She looked at Molly who didn't seem to have a clue she was nearly knocked out cold by the errant ball.

"Hey…nice catch."

Hailey turned towards the deep voice. It was the third baseman who'd tried to make a play on the ball before it drifted out of range and into the stands. He smiled at her and gave her a thumbs up. He was 6'5" of pure hunkiness. Dark blond hair, hazel eyes, square jaw, broad shoulders and one big, brilliant smile. Hailey began to feel as if *she* had been plunked by the ball: lightheaded and goofy.

"Thank you," she mumbled as she broke out into a smile, she could feel her cheeks flush.

"Hello…earth to Hailey." Molly waived her hand in front of her eyes. "Snap out of it."

"What? I'm fine. I just saved you from a trip to the hospital for your information," Hailey said as she handed the foul ball to the young girl sitting behind her.

"I think you caught more than a ball," Molly said, a smirk on her face, nodding her chin towards the third baseman.

"No I didn't. He was just being nice. That's all."

"Just being nice? That was more than just being nice. The guy—the smoking *hot guy*—was practically drooling over you."

"Yeah, right. These guys have a million women lined up. It was nothing." But *she* had felt a little something in her stomach when he smiled at her. Actually, more than a *little* something, it felt like a thunderbolt had ripped through her. She discreetly found his name in her program: #25 Matt Harper. She kept staring at him from behind her sunglasses. Was it her imagination, or did he just turn and smile at her as he ran back to the dugout? Now it looked as if he was gesturing towards her as he talked to one of his teammates. "Hey, let me borrow those." She kept her gaze focused on him as she reached for the binoculars that were still firmly glued to Molly's face.

"No...I've got number fifty-five finally in focus." Molly wrenched the glasses from Hailey's grip.

She looked over at the dugout again. It definitely looked like he was pointing towards her.

"Seriously Molls...let me have them." Hailey turned and grabbed them with both hands, Molly tightened her grip on them as they began to wrestle over the binoculars. "Give 'em."

"No!"

They continued to struggle over them until Hailey gave one big final yank and wrenched them free from her friend's grip. Unfortunately this also caused the nachos in Molly's lap to become airborne, landing on the guy seated in front of them.

"What the hell?" He turned around angrily.

"I'm so sorry," Hailey said half-heartedly as she desperately tried to focus in on the third baseman. She could hear Molly snickering next to her.

"I'm moving to a different seat," the guy said. "I'm tired of listening to the two of you yick yack during the game. And now *this*." He gestured to the unnaturally orange cheese sauce covering one shoulder and sleeve of his t-shirt. He shook his head as he gathered his things.

"Oh yeah? At least we don't put ketchup on our hot dog," Molly yelled after him.

"Molls...are we *condiment* shaming people now?" Hailey put the binoculars down.

"If you're over the age of six and still put ketchup on your hot dog, then yeah, you're going to get condiment shamed."

Hailey was only half listening as she looked for the third baseman. *Matt.* She sighed aloud and let a smile fall over her face. Lucky for her there was no chance in hell she'd be crossing paths with the likes of him. She didn't think she'd have the willpower to stick to her new "no-guys" rule if he were on the menu.

CHAPTER TWO

ITTING ON A PITCH: A batter who is waiting for a particular type of pitch before swinging at it.

Rob's concentration was interrupted by the sound of soft whimpering. He looked down at the small dog sitting patiently in the dog bed.

"Okay Sandy, we're going soon. I promise." He began to gather the files spread out on his desk, tucking them into the soft leather briefcase that had been a gift from his grandparents after he graduated from law school. He loved being able to dog-sit for Hailey whenever she was out of town. He would love to have a dog of his own someday, but even in his pet-friendly office it was often a challenge to take care of Sandy and attend to his job as a sports agent, which often included wining and dining clients or prospective clients. It also involved 60-hour work weeks and a good deal of travel. All of which were not ideal conditions for dog ownership, or dog parenthood as Hailey would say.

He wasn't complaining, he had been lucky enough to land his dream job. He wasn't just *any* sports agent, but a *baseball* sports agent, a sport he had been in love with since he was a small boy.

As he gathered up Sandy's bed and hooked the leash onto the dog's collar, he felt his phone buzz.

Mom: Don't be late...your grandfather is already looking tired and the brisket is at risk of drying out.

Rob: No worries, we're on our way.

He headed towards the parking garage, his arms full with Sandy's bed and his briefcase.

"Get ready for some spoiling, you're going to see Grandma Ruth." He looked down at the small dog who looked up at him, his thin, shoestring-like tail wagging madly. Rob's grandmother adored Sandy and always fed him an assortment of delicacies. In return, Sandy adored Grandma Ruth.

As soon as he walked through the door of his childhood home, Rob was welcomed by the intoxicating aroma of home cooked food.

"Hi sweetie," his mom said. She pulled Rob in for a warm hug and a kiss on the cheek before turning her attention to Sandy. "I better say hello now before Grandma Ruth gets a hold of you," she said as she scratched the dog behind his ears.

"Robbie, sweetheart, how are you?" Rob's grandmother opened her arms wide for a hug. He was always shocked that such a tiny woman could give such a death grip of a bear hug.

"I'm fine grandma, you smell really good." Rob stood back and looked at the stylish woman. She was wearing winter white pants and a black silk blouse with a bold gold necklace. His grandmother was always the picture of quiet elegance.

"It's new, it's from Annabelle Grande," she said with a big smile.

"Mom, it's *Ariana* Grande." Rob's mom softly smiled and shook her head before going back to her cooking.

"You're wearing Ariana Grande perfume?" Rob asked, his eyebrows raised in surprise.

"Just because I'm old doesn't mean I have to *smell* like I'm old." Rob's grandma scooped Sandy up in her arms. "I've got a completely dog friendly Passover treat for you my little boychik." She planted several kisses on the dog's head while Sandy wagged his tail in utter bliss.

"Don't give him too much, Grandma. I don't want him throwing up in my car on the way home."

"Tssk...just a little chopped liver, *without onions*, and some matzo balls. He'll be fine...he's Jewish after all." She tucked the dog under one arm.

"Grandma, the dog isn't Jewish...he's a *dog*." Rob watched as she turned towards him.

"Did you see the way he ate the noodle kugel last time he was here? *And*, he's named after the greatest Jewish athlete of all time. The dog is Jewish Robbie." With that she left the kitchen.

Rob's mom nudged him in the side with her elbow while she continued to stir the sauce on the stove. "Let her have her fun...we both know the dog isn't Jewish since Hailey isn't." His mom gave him a wink. Before he could protest, she continued. "Speaking of Hailey, how's it going? I'm guessing you haven't said anything to her."

Rob had spilled his guts to his mom about his feelings for Hailey after one too many glasses of champagne at his cousin Mark's wedding a month earlier. He had gushed like a baby about how he had been pining for her since they had met. His mom wouldn't let the subject drop and kept asking when he was going to talk to Hailey.

And he *had* been pining for her. He'd been pining over Hailey since the second he had rescued her from the library and listened while she sobbed over some creep who'd hurt her. Rob could have made a move right then and there; she was vulnerable, and he was the knight there to rescue her. But that wasn't how he operated. He had been raised differently than that. He had been raised to be a gentleman. A *mensch* in Yiddish was someone of great integrity and honor. His dad and grandfather were menschen and Rob aspired to be considered one too. But sometimes Rob had to wonder whether he was losing the distinction between gentleman and doormat. He certainly didn't want to be perceived as a wimp, that was the last thing he was.

He had wanted to ask Hailey out once she was over the jerk who made her cry in the library. But before that could happen she had moved on to the next guy. It seemed Rob never had a chance to get his foot in the door. She was either in a new relationship or he was consoling her over said relationship going belly-up. Before he knew it, they had moved towards being good friends. He then worried about making it "weird" if he told her how he felt if she didn't feel the same way. Their friendship had become far too important to him to risk it.

"No, I haven't said anything to her, Mom." He stole a piece of the brisket sitting under foil, resting on a platter.

"Don't you think you should?" She looked at him with that knowing way she had, as she continued to stir the sauce. Not missing a beat.

"When's David getting here?" Rob tried not so subtly to change to topic.

"Your brother and Hannah will be here in about 30 minutes. Don't change the topic on me Robert."

"Robert? Sounds like I'm in trouble." He smiled and gave his mom a squeeze of her shoulders. "I promise I'll talk to her soon." He kissed the top of her head.

"Talk to who soon? And who's in trouble?" His grandpa

Charlie walked into the kitchen, resting heavily on the cane in his hand. "And when's dinner? By the time we get through the Seder I'm going to be famished. What am I saying? I'm already famished."

Rob discreetly passed him a chunk of brisket. His grandpa winked at him as he chewed on the piece of meat.

"I'm guessing you're the one in trouble Rob. Who are you supposed to be talking to?" Although his grandfather was approaching 80 years of age, he still looked healthy and vibrant despite the bad hip. He always had a twinkle in his eye and a smile on his face.

"I…it's…umm…" Rob shifted his weight.

"It's Hailey…Robbie's in love with her." Grandma Ruth had returned to the kitchen, Sandy following close on her heels.

"Mom…I asked you not to tell anyone," Rob groaned as he hung his head down, staring at his loafers.

"She didn't tell me anything…I just knew." His grandma shrugged her shoulders and raised her eyebrows. "But you should have told me," she said as she turned towards Rob's mom.

"Hey everyone, sorry we're late."

"David!" His mother turned from her cooking to hug Rob's older brother. She then planted a kiss on his wife Hannah's cheek. "You look beautiful, dear." She smiled at the tall brunette.

"So do you Lois, as always." Hannah set down the bottles of wine in her hands.

"You know you can call me Mom," Rob's mom said as she turned the stove off and poured the sauce into a dish.

"Mom, that's so old world…no one does that." David pulled his mom in for a big hug.

"How's my baby brother?" David grabbed one of Rob's

shoulders with one hand and pulled him in for a hug with the other. "Land a big leaguer yet?"

"No…not yet, but I've got some double-A prospects that I think could hit the bigs."

Rob looked at his older brother. David had the same brown hair as his, soft curls and all. Although Rob was no slouch in the height department, David stood a good three inches taller, he had shoulders like a linebacker and hands like a quarterback. He'd played baseball in college and was good enough to be courted by the pros, but he turned his back on it to go to medical school and become an orthopedic surgeon. The whole family was proud of David. Rob sometimes felt like he was in his older brother's shadow, whatever David had done Rob had tried. When it came to sports, he was only average in skill though. So, he had stuck his head into his studies and went to law school.

"Okay, everyone into the dining room," his mom said, as she ushered everyone out of the kitchen.

❦

"Dinner was good, Mom." Rob stacked the plate he was drying on top of the others on the counter.

"Thank you, sweetie. Would you make sure to help your grandparents out to their car. I'm always afraid that Dad will fall with that hip of his."

"Of course." Rob kissed his mom on the top of the head and hung up the dish towel he'd been holding.

"I don't need any help," Rob's grandfather announced as he pulled his coat on.

"Oh, stop being so stubborn," his grandmother chided her husband gently.

"Grandpa it's no trouble." Rob walked with his grandparents out to their car. He helped Ruth in the car and walked around to the driver's side with his grandfather.

"Look here Rob. Why wait for something to happen with this girl...if you feel that way about her, tell her. You'll regret it the rest of your life if you don't." His grandfather had a twinkle in his eye as he held Rob's gaze, one hand on his shoulder, the other on his cane.

"But what if she doesn't feel the same and what if it then ruins our friendship?" Rob looked into his grandfather's gray eyes for answers.

"Would you rather stay friends and watch her meet someone else? Marry someone else? I guess you can always go to her wedding as a friend." He looked at Rob with a serious look. "When you find the woman you think is for you, then you have to make a move before someone else does."

Rob looked down at his shoes before looking back up at his grandfather. "Maybe you're right," he said, holding the car door open while his grandfather climbed in. "Good luck with your surgery, Grandpa; I'm going to come see you as soon as you can have visitors. Bye Grandma Ruth." Rob shut the car door and watched the red taillights disappear.

He stood outside for a bit, pondering what his grandfather had said. The thought of Hailey meeting someone and getting married made him wince. The truth was, he didn't think he could watch her become someone else's wife, it would be too painful. She was perfect for him. He was enormously attracted to her. He had been from the moment he laid eyes on her. They talked about baseball, books, and life in general. And they took care of one another. When Rob took his bar exam, a grueling multi-day experience, Hailey had done everything in her power to support him. She'd stocked his refrigerator full of healthy foods, she'd cleaned his apartment, made lunches and snacks for him to take to the exam center, and had tried to distract him with Sandy and Netflix while he counted down the hours to the test results. Isn't that what you hoped for in a partner?

What am I waiting for? His friend Jon from college was getting married the next month. Why not ask Hailey to be his plus one? He took out his phone and texted her before he could chicken out.

Rob: Hey Hailey...how's Arizona? Just checking to confirm that I'm still picking you and Molly up from LAX tomorrow at 5:30.

He watched as the three familiar dots began to move.

Hailey: Thank you!!!! Yes...tomorrow at 5:30...we'll meet you at the curb by the northwest terminal. Arizona is great! Can't wait to see Sandy...I hope he's been good for you.

Rob: He's great. My grandma made him some kosher dog treats and he loved it.

Hailey: Aww...that's so sweet...she really loves him.

Rob: He loves her too. Btw...I've got something to ask you tomorrow after we drop Molly off. Maybe we can go grab something to eat?

Hailey: Sure! I've got something to tell you also. Gotta go, we're just going in to eat.

Rob: Ok...say hi to Molly for me.

Hailey: :-)

Rob took a deep breath. No backing out now. He wondered what Hailey wanted to talk to him about. He shoved his hands into his pockets and walked back inside.

〰

Rob pulled his car up to the curb at the LAX arrivals area. He spotted Hailey and Molly immediately. His heart always caught a bit when he laid eyes on Hailey. Seeing her never failed to put a smile on his face. He got out of the car and walked up to her with Sandy in his arms.

"Sandy!" Hailey yelled, her face breaking into a wide grin. "Rob!" she said with a bit less enthusiasm.

"Now I know how I rate against the dog," Rob said, followed by a sly smile.

"Oh knock it off," Hailey said, elbowing him in the ribs as she took Sandy from his arms. "I missed my little guy."

"Well now I hope you're talking about the dog," Rob said as Hailey pulled him in for a hug. He inhaled her scent of oranges and vanilla. She always smelled so damn good.

"Ha ha, funny," Hailey said, giving Rob a playful push on the shoulder.

He loaded their luggage into the car and slipped in behind the steering wheel.

"So how was Arizona?" he asked, looking at Molly in his rear-view mirror as he pulled away from the curb.

"Awesome," Molly said. "So many hot guys...how did I not know this about baseball?" She shook her head as she scrolled through her phone.

Hot guys???

"The baseball was awesome," Hailey said. "Thanks for hooking us up with tickets, Rob. We had great seats at every game."

"Sure thing," he replied. He stole a glance at Hailey's tanned and shapely legs. He felt the familiar longing begin in his core. *Eyes on the road, Rob.* Clearing his throat with a cough, he glanced at Molly in the mirror. "Text me your address," he said as he pulled out of LAX and onto the freeway.

CHAPTER THREE

MENDOZA LINE: *A batting average of .200. Named (most likely) for Mario Mendoza, a notoriously poor hitter but decent shortstop.*

"Do you mind if we grab some tacos at that place near my apartment? I'm starved and they have that outdoor area so we can bring Sandy with us." Hailey looked over at Rob. The sight of him always brought a smile to her face. He was a good and constant friend, she felt lucky to have him in her life. She couldn't understand why he was single. He was hot, smart, funny, kind, and had a good and interesting job. It didn't make any sense. Maybe he just didn't share that part of his life with her. *Could that be?* She didn't think that was it, but it was still a mystery to her why he was available. Had he expressed any interest beyond being friends, Hailey would have jumped at the chance to be something more to him. But she had long ago given up hope of anything more.

They placed their order and found a table outside in the patio area. The weather was a perfect Los Angeles seventy-five degrees, the sky was beginning its transformation as the sun slowly headed west. She gave Sandy a cup of water before turning to Rob.

"So, I wanted to ask…" Rob began.

"Wait…I have to tell you *my* news first," Hailey said excitedly. She looked at Rob, his soft brown curls framed his chocolate brown eyes.

"Okay," Rob replied.

She took a deep breath and blew it out slowly through pursed lips.

"I've made a decision…I'm off men." She looked at him, seeing a look of surprise on his face.

"Wait…what does that mean? Are you *on* women?" Rob pushed on the bridge of his tortoise shell framed glasses. Was it shock or confusion that she was reading on his face?

"Not women, silly. I just mean that I need to take a hiatus from men and relationships. A *real* break. You know my track record. I can't seem to trust my own heart or my head these days…or ever. You know what bad luck with guys I've had. It's time to take a break and 'find myself' so to speak." She used air quotes. "At least my therapist thinks it's a good idea."

She had finally decided to try to figure out why her relationships were so short-lived. She actually had a feeling she knew *why*. She just had to figure out the *how*. How to stop sabotaging herself and how to stop looking to men to fill the void in her soul. She had called her therapist so they could begin twice weekly sessions until Hailey felt whole. If that made any sense. She took a sip of her water and waited for him to respond. His face was stoic, or in other words: a normal Rob face.

"Well? Aren't you going to say anything?" she asked.

Just then the server placed their order down on the table. Hailey wasted no time digging into her chicken and avocado taco. She plucked some chicken out for Sandy who quickly took the morsels from her fingers.

"I, I don't know what to say." Rob rubbed a hand over his jaw before picking up a taco. "Seems kind of extreme," he replied in between bites.

"It's hardly extreme. Lots of people take breaks from dating when it isn't working. And for me it's totally not working. I seem to be batting below the Mendoza line when it comes to love." She wiped her mouth with a paper napkin before taking a sip of water.

Rob chuckled. "You need to find a guy who loves baseball as much as you do." His eyes looked up at her.

"Yeah, maybe...not sure that would make a difference." She finished her second taco before remembering that Rob said he had something to talk about. "So, what's your big news? I've been bellyaching about my love life and forgot you said you had something to tell me...or ask me." She looked at him and picked up a clean napkin, leaning across the table to wipe the hot sauce from his chin.

"Thanks," he said to her.

"No problem, that's what friends are for."

Rob cleared his throat. "Do you want to be my plus one for a wedding? My friend Jon is getting married next month. The wedding is in Santa Monica."

"Sure," Hailey replied. "I'd love to."

"It's black tie."

"Great, I have a new dress that has had no occasion to be worn." She snorted. "It's been a sad reminder that my love life sucks...I swear it mocks me every time I see it."

"Great. I'll email you the details."

They finished their food and talked about baseball. Rob drove her and Sandy to her apartment and helped carry her luggage in, making sure they were settled. He had even offered to run to the store and stock her fridge for her. He really was a best friend. Hailey smiled to herself.

CHAPTER FOUR

FIVE O'CLOCK HITTER: *A hitter who hits really well during batting practice, but not so well during games.*

"Okay, so let me get this straight. You finally decide to make a move with Hailey but before you can, she tells you she's off men"? Rob's friend Spencer pulled his tee from the grass and stuffed his driver back into his golf bag.

"That about sums it up," Rob replied as he lined up his golf ball looking down the fairway. He had left the office early to catch a round of golf with his friend from grade school. Spencer worked as a UPS driver. He worked Saturdays, which meant he had a weekday off, the perfect time to get in 18 holes of golf.

"Fore!" Rob yelled as his shot took a wicked slice. "Shit," he muttered as he put his club away and got behind the wheel of the golf cart.

"I still don't get why you can't just tell her how you feel. She's been in between boyfriends more times than you slice that tee shot," Spencer teased.

Rob had pondered this many times himself. He'd just never gotten any vibe from Hailey that she felt the same.

He'd only ever gotten the friend vibe. Maybe his radar was off, but he didn't think so. He'd seen Hailey practically throw herself at men she was interested in. "I've been hesitant partially because she's never indicated at all that she feels the same about me."

"*Girls* don't make the first move, we do." Spencer looked over at him.

"First, at this point in our lives it's 'women' not girls, and second, that's some kind of 1950's sexist nonsense," Rob said.

Spencer shrugged his shoulders. "Maybe. But it's true."

Rob looked over at his friend. Spencer had an easy way about him, a California surfer dude crossed with Brad Pitt. Shaggy blond hair, blue eyes and a year-round tan. "Hey, how about you join us and her friend Molly for a night out? It would make it easier for me. I could get a foot in the door so to speak without it seeming too weird to her."

Spencer furrowed his brow. "Molly? Is that the one who plays tennis?"

"Yeah," Rob replied, feeling hopeful.

"Forget it." Spencer said as he slid out of the cart and walked to his ball, waiting for Rob to hit his ball since Rob's tee shot was short of his.

"What do you mean? She's attractive…she's an athlete, that should be right up your alley, man." Rob selected his club as he glanced over at his friend.

"I know she's attractive. *Very.*" Spencer replied. A corner of his mouth twitched.

Rob took his shot, the ball landed in the sand trap. "Fuck." He shook his head as he headed back to the cart. "You've met her? When?"

"At that party you had a couple of summers ago. She walked straight up to me, took one look at my Spider Man t-shirt, and said, 'what are you…twelve?'" Spencer shook his head, landing his shot about a foot from the hole.

"Yikes, that's harsh," Rob replied.

"Tell me about it. When I told her it was the only thing that was clean, she said, 'that's even worse' and walked off. So, yeah, thanks but no thanks. You're on your own."

Rob grabbed a sand wedge and headed over to the trap. "Hailey's my plus one at Jon's wedding next month." He landed his shot on the green. The ball picking up speed, rolled ten feet past the hole.

"Bingo, there's your answer," Spencer said, his eyebrows up, a smile on his face. "Chicks dig weddings. They get all weepy and shit, plus add in some champagne and she'll be all over you before the cake is cut. I guarantee it."

Rob lined up his putt. "That's hardly how I want to make my move, with an emotionally weakened and inebriated Hailey." He sank the long putt. "Finally," he said under his breath.

"It's up to you, man. I'm just telling you that a romantic wedding is the perfect time to make your move with her."

Rob silently thought about this. Maybe Spencer was on to something. But he wanted Hailey in her right mind, not awash with the hormones that it seemed, according to Spencer at least, a wedding triggered in women. *Did it?* We'll be dressed up, it's at a romantic location, it's a wedding so it's all about love. Maybe. Just maybe.

He wasn't sure why he hadn't been able to tell Hailey how he felt about her. If this was David, he would have already taken the proverbial bull by the horns. No questions asked. It wasn't that Rob was soft or weak. He had been known to be quite hardball when it came to negotiating contracts for his clients. But with Hailey, he hadn't been able to find the courage. He was so frightened of scaring her away. He needed to keep her in his life. But he didn't want to end up in the place where it was *her* wedding he'd be attending. He needed to talk to her. Soon.

"Hey, I'm glad we could meet," Hailey said to him. She gave him a big hug. Her faint vanilla and orange scent grabbed his senses. It was almost painful pulling away from her, he wanted to linger in her scent...in her orbit. They had met up at the dog park near his office. He brought a couple of sandwiches from the nearby bakery, sliced turkey on fresh, hot sourdough rolls. The day was sunny and warm, and the dog park was fairly busy. They sat on a bench in the shade watching Sandy nose around at something in the bushes. Being around Hailey was always easy. To Rob it felt like two puzzle pieces coming together.

"So, we're all set for this weekend, right?" He took a bite of sandwich and looked over at her. She had her blond hair tucked behind one ear as she chewed, nodding her head. Just that simple movement made his heart beat faster.

"Yep. What time are you picking me up?" She opened the bag of chips sitting between them.

"Say, around 4? The traffic getting there is unpredictable."

"Sounds good. I'll be ready." She wiped her face with a napkin and took a sip from her water bottle.

"How's work?"

"Good, I have a new client. She writes cozy mysteries and wants a new editor. My a/c has been on the fritz, so I've been working at the library. Landlord said he'd have it fixed by tomorrow...downside to working from home I guess."

"Are you telling me it's not all pajamas and ice cream," Rob laughed, looking over at her.

"Ninety percent it is." Hailey looked at him and winked. "Hey, did you get a chance to read that book I gave you? The one about spies?"

"Oh, yeah. I meant to say something about it. You were right, it was good. It felt like a fiction thriller, not like real

25

life. Can you imagine being that guy? I would have been terrified."

"Me too. I'm glad you liked it. The first clue that the head of the agency was no good was when they mentioned that he didn't like dogs. I mean, bingo. It's a bad guy if they don't like dogs or if the dog doesn't like them."

Just then Sandy came running over, a small doodle on his heels.

"Hey, cutie. What's your name?" Hailey asked as she gave the curly coated dog a scratch on the head. The dog's eyes were focused like a laser on her sandwich. A tall, lanky young guy came running up.

"Bear, it's time to go," he said to the dog. "Cute dog you have," he said, pointing his chin towards Sandy as he attached Bear's leash to his collar. "What's your name?" He gave Sandy a pet along his back.

"Sandy," Hailey replied.

"Hi Sandy, you're a good girl," the guy said in a comically baby voice.

"He," Hailey said.

Uh oh, here we go, thought Rob to himself. He'd witnessed this scene before. Hailey was about to go berserk if this guy wasn't careful.

"He?" The guy said, a quizzical look on his face as he looked back from Sandy to Hailey. "I thought you said her name was Sandy."

"*His* name *is* Sandy. As in *Sandy Koufax*. The greatest person to ever wear the Dodger uniform. How can you even be from around here and not know that?" Hailey's voice was rising.

"Sheesh," the guy said under his breath as he walked away. His dog Bear in tow.

"Uh, maybe go a bit easier on people who aren't familiar

with Koufax," Rob said. He was trying to hold down a laugh that wanted to bubble up to the surface.

"Seriously? I mean really, how can anyone consider themselves an Angeleno and not be familiar with Sandy Koufax? How?" Hailey shook her head as she gathered up her sandwich trash.

"Cut him some slack, it's not like the guy didn't know who Randy Johnson was…the greatest lefty ever. No. Strike that. The greatest *pitcher* ever." Rob smiled to himself as he brushed sandwich crumbs from his lap.

"Oh, not this again," Hailey groaned. "I'm not sure I have the energy for this discussion today when it's clear that the greatest pitcher ever is Sandy Koufax, righty *or* lefty."

"At his peak, maybe. But you gotta give it to Johnson when you consider the length of their careers," Rob said.

"Argh!" Hailey playfully pushed Rob on the shoulder.

"I'm just teasing you," he said. He reached down and fed Sandy a bit of turkey he'd set aside from his sandwich. He looked at Hailey and felt his heart swell. Not an uncommon occurrence when he was around her.

"I've got to get back to work," Hailey said, standing up. "The mystery writer gave me a really short deadline, so we'll need to table this debate." She gave him a wink.

"No problem. I'll see you Saturday at four." They hugged. Rob tried to hold on to her scent as he walked back to the office.

CHAPTER FIVE

*A*DVANCE *A RUNNER: To move a runner ahead safely to another base, often the conscious strategy of a team that plays small ball. If a batter does make an out, his plate appearance will have been less negative if he still got a runner into scoring position; in certain situations, batters even deliberately sacrifice themselves.*

"I Jonathan, take you Emily, to be my best friend and lover. I promise to always take care of you when you are sick or when you are just having a bad day. I promise from the bottom of my heart to always be here for you, and I promise to love you until my time on earth is no more."

Oh my God, oh my God, oh my God. Do not cry. Do not cry! Ugh. Think about that triple play you saw last night.

Although Hailey was trying her very best not to lose her ever loving shit and bawl like a baby as Rob's plus one, tears began to roll down her cheeks. She should have known this would happen. She was twenty-seven years old and was nowhere near being able to ever see herself get married and have children. Yes. She said it. She wanted to have children. She loved children despite the horrible childhood she'd had. A big part of her yearned so desperately to have a big happy family with a loving husband by her side. A house with a white picket fence crawling with kids and dogs. Something to help erase what had gone on in her own childhood. She often wondered whether she *would* be a good mother. She certainly hadn't had a good role model. She made herself stop thinking these thoughts. *Pull it together, Hailey.* She brushed the tears from her cheeks with the back of her hand.

She stole a glance at Rob. He looked so damn handsome in his tuxedo she thought as she admired his profile. *He* would make a good husband. Even though Rob could be somewhat stoic at times, he had all the qualities that she wanted in a spouse: strong but gentle, tough but tender, cute but sexy. Loved dogs and baseball. Smart, funny, well-read, and he had a close-knit and loving family. He was solid. He would definitely make some woman or… man…because she couldn't rule out Rob being gay…very happy. He literally had never talked about dating anyone with her. Ever. Whenever she brought the subject up, he abruptly changed it. It was the one area of his life which wasn't shared. She really didn't know what to make of it. Rob just always changed the subject and murmured something about being too busy with work. Whatever the case, man or woman, Rob would make someone very happy someday. He was perfect husband material.

Rob nudged her shoulder with his and mouthed "are you okay?" His brown eyes were full of concern. For some reason, maybe it was being at a wedding, but she felt a little niggling of butterflies in her stomach as she looked at him, more than usual…and she had the irresistible urge to run her hands through his soft brown hair. She nodded that she was fine.

"That was nice," Rob said. He handed her a glass of champagne. Cocktails and hors-d'oeuvres were being served after the ceremony outdoors on the hotel's balcony overlooking the Pacific Ocean. The sun had just dipped below the horizon and the sky was turning from blue to orange with dark pink and purple streaks running across it. Hailey took a sip of her drink. *Why am I feeling so emotional?* For some reason, the combination of the wedding ceremony, her recent string of failed relationships, and Rob on her arm looking completely hot and tending to her like she was the only person in the world, was all combining to turn her into one big emotional blob. *Pull it together, Hailey.*

"It was," she replied. "They look so in love." She smiled and looked down at her champagne.

Rob nodded in response as he sipped his drink. "Yeah, I'm happy for him."

What was it she was seeing in his eyes? Sadness? Wistfulness? Or was he just bored? Didn't most guys hate going to weddings?

She looked at him. "Did you see that triple play last night? The Dodgers and Giants?"

A tuxedoed server came by with a tray of bacon-wrapped scallops. Rob took two, handing one to Hailey.

"Shit, yeah. That was awesome. Good win for our guys," Rob said. A smile washed over his face and his body looked as if it had completely relaxed. As long as they could talk baseball, the world was good again.

After cocktails, they feasted on a four-course, sit down meal. Hailey had sole with beurre Blanc sauce, tender green beans, jasmine rice and a little gems salad. It was a top-notch meal. The band began to play, and couples moved to the dance floor. Hailey had had a few glasses of wine with her meal and was feeling the effects of having slightly fewer inhibitions. When she looked at Rob, she felt the familiar flutters in her stomach and a warmth spread through her body. Sometimes it confused her. They were friends and did things for each other that friends do. Like the time she practically took up residence in the bathroom with a nasty bout of food poisoning. Rob had been there. He had held her hair back as she vomited into the toilet. He'd gently wiped her face with a cool washcloth. Brought her ginger ale and ice cubes to suck on. He brought her won ton soup from Chinatown once she was feeling better. His grandmother had told him it was a miracle curing soup. He slept on her couch for two nights, taking care of both Sandy and her.

"Let's dance," she said to Rob, gently pulling on his arm. She couldn't quite read his face. Was it discomfort she saw or awkwardness? Did he even dance? "C'mon…it will be fun…I promise." She gave him a wink and grabbed both his hands in hers and gently pulled him from his chair.

The song was slow. Rob pulled her close to him, his hands around her waist. She placed her head in the crook between his chin and his chest; shutting her eyes she took a breath slowly in. He smelled of soap, and something manly…like leather and spices. They danced quietly together. The warmth from his body crossed over into hers, making her feel at home. She felt she could stay there forever. Just as she was nearly dozing off in a Zen, dreamlike state, the music turned upbeat. Rob took a step back and looked at her through thick lashes. If she didn't know better, she would swear she saw desire in his eyes. *How much has he had to drink?* She was pretty sure he'd had only one glass of wine with dinner. He took her by the hand and in a low voice said, "let's go outside for a bit."

Once the salty night air hit her in the face, Hailey woke up from her daze. Rob softly placed his hand on the small of her back, guiding her to the railing overlooking the beach below. She could see him swallow hard. Maybe she wasn't imagining what was going on between them. She studied the lines of his jaw as they curved towards his lips. She'd always been drawn to his looks. Rob was a very handsome guy in a boyish way, and she always felt a bit of a twinge in her stomach whenever he was near.

How had they always stayed in the friend zone? Was it that he wasn't interested in *that* way? Or was it something else? Had she given off only "friend" vibes all these years? She did seem to nearly always be either in or just out of a relationship. Maybe that turned him off. But one thing that hadn't been turned off was their friendship. She cared a lot about him and treasured what they had together.

They stood side by side, watching the waves come and go, neither one of them saying a word. Hailey's shoulder rested against Rob's arm. If she wasn't so tipsy, she would swear she could feel something close to an electrical current running between them. Back and forth in an unbroken arc. She turned towards him, wanting to see if she could detect anything in his eyes.

Rob turned towards her. The warmth of his body was setting hers on fire. She could see his Adam's apple move up and down. His eyes, dark chocolate brown framed by dark lashes, were half-lidded as he looked at her. She swallowed hard. Her heart was racing right up her throat. Maybe he *did* have more than friend feelings for her after all, she thought as she stood on weak legs.

Rob put a hand on the small of her back and began to speak. "Hailey, I, uh, I want to talk to you about some—"

Just then one of the bridesmaids came out to the balcony and announced that the cake was about to be cut. She smiled at them and gestured for them to come inside. Hailey looked at Rob, he shook his head before taking her by the hand and leading her back inside.

Later that night, back at her apartment, Hailey had returned from walking Sandy for his evening business. She took some aspirin and vitamin C tablets with a big glass of water in hopes of staving off any kind of a hangover the next morning. Probably wishful thinking. As she stood brushing her teeth she thought back over the evening with Rob. Her feelings were all mixed up like a salad. On the one hand Rob was a friend, always had been. Perhaps it was just the wedding romance vibes spilling over into things. But she knew she had felt *something* between them that couldn't just be chalked up to wedding hormones. It started while they were dancing. A different kind of connection to Rob could be felt, different than anything she had ever experienced with him.

She never got anything more than friend feelings from him. Until tonight, at least. She'd never wanted to stick her neck out and make a move with him. Didn't guys usually do that? In Hailey's experience they did. *If* they were interested.

When she drilled down into it, Rob was very different than the kind of guy she involved herself with romantically. She usually went for the overtly cocky and slightly arrogant frat boy type. It never lasted. But why? Why hadn't she ever gone out with the strong and silent, nice guy type such as Rob? Part of it, she was certain, was due to her childhood. She was always, usually unconsciously, looking to quickly fill in the gaps in her soul that needed instant affirmation that she was wanted. But what she usually got was lustful desire that she confused with love.

She climbed into bed and took a shaky breath in, slowly letting it out while she stroked Sandy's silky coat. The dog looked up at her with his brown eyes and gave her a lick on the hand, as if he could read her mind. She leaned down and kissed him on his head.

"I love you, Sandy."

The dog replied with a wag of his tail. She slid under the comforter and snapped the light off next to her. She soon fell into a deep sleep.

CHAPTER SIX

*C*UP OF COFFEE: *A short time spent by a minor league player at the major league level. The idea is that the player was there only long enough to have a cup of coffee.*

"You're *what?*" Spencer's face was incredulous as he chewed on his Kobe beef hot dog.

"I'm going to meet with Matt Harper and try to convince him to stay with the firm. Specifically, to let *me* represent him." Rob grabbed an onion ring from the tray sitting between them. They were at their favorite pub for dinner before watching the Dodgers play the Padres on one of the big screen televisions around them.

"How? Doesn't Dan Silverman represent him?" Spencer's eyes were wide with surprise as he grabbed his beer to wash down his food.

"Well, he did. He was in Tanzania on a safari and was killed. By a hippo." Rob felt sadness over Dan's death, even though he was a mean, cutthroat son of a bitch and not a fun guy to work for. But still. He had a wife and kids, and for them especially Rob was sad.

"You're shitting me. A *hippo* killed him?" Spencer wiped his hands off on a wad of napkins, letting them fall onto his plate. "What the fuck?"

Rob took a sip of his beer and sat it down in front of him. "Yeah. Evidently hippos kill more people than any other animal," Rob said. "Who knew?"

"No shit." Spencer shook his head. "Note to self, stick to the zoo."

"The firm is assigning his clients to anyone and everyone, trying to get them all to stay and not jump ship to one of the other firms. I got dealt Matt Harper. I'm going to meet with him this weekend while they're in Chicago playing the Cubs." He ran a thumb through the condensation on his glass. "But that's only half of my news."

"Oh yeah? What's the other half?" asked Spencer as he flagged down the server for another round of beers.

"I'm going to ask Hailey to go with me. I figured it would be a good time to tell her how I feel. You know, just me and her. Good seats to the game, take her to a fantastic restaurant and then…lay it all out. It's time." Rob took a deep breath and leaned back against the booth. He'd played out the scenario a million times in his head and had seen it going a million different ways in the past. But now he felt more confident as to how it would all shake out. He was taking a page from his brother's book and not letting the fear of failure stop him this time. After the wedding he'd decided it was time to come clean with Hailey. Lay his cards out and see where they landed. He'd come so close to kissing her that night while they were standing outside. He thought she might feel the same. Maybe. There had been a chemistry between them while they danced, it had felt like a current running between their two bodies. Her body language told him that maybe she had felt it too, and he didn't think it was all chalked up to "wedding hormones" as Spencer had suggested or to the champagne. He wanted to tell her how he felt. But he was nervous. No, not nervous, downright scared.

What if she didn't feel the same way? What if she truly only saw him as a friend? What if she wasn't attracted to him? He'd make a fool of himself, and more importantly, he'd risk their friendship. It was possible Hailey would disappear from his life. The 'what ifs' were playing with his head, but he'd decided that one of these outcomes would be far less painful than watching her meet her "happily ever after" person; so, he was ready. It was time.

"Wow. Good for you, man. That's huge. I'm glad you're finally going to tell her. Because one of these days, she's going to meet someone she'll stick with, and then where will you be?" Spencer bit into an onion ring. "Watching her marry someone else will haunt you for the rest of your life."

Rob felt an ugly sensation move down his body at just the thought of that. Good thing he was finally making his move.

❦

"Rob, this is beautiful!" Hailey was beaming from ear to ear as she looked out the window of the hotel. The room was on the 40th floor and had an expansive view of Lake Michigan. "I can't believe your firm is paying for *both* of us to stay here!" She turned to look at him. He was leaning against the wall, hands in his pockets. He pushed his glasses up with this finger.

"Yep. They're desperate to keep Dan's clients." Actually, Rob had paid for Hailey's flight and her room, but he didn't want to tell her that. At least not yet.

"That's so awful. A *hippo* for Pete's sake. I always thought they were so cute. I even had a stuffed one when I was little." She shuddered.

"Yeah, who knew?" Rob shrugged his shoulders. "I have a meeting tonight, down at the hotel bar. But then I'll be free. I made dinner reservations at this really great place in Lincoln Park. Handmade pasta, fresh ingredients…it's supposed to be fantastic."

"Yum, sounds great. What time?" Hailey opened her suitcase and began to put her clothes away.

"Nine…I hope that's not too late?"

"Nope…that's seven back home…not too late at all." She hung up the red dress she was planning to wear. She heard Rob clear his throat and looked up to see his eyes on the sleeveless garment. "Are you okay? Do you need some water or something?" Hailey eyed him, her hands on her hips.

"No, I'm fine. I'm going to go unpack. We'll have some time to walk around before my meeting. Sound good?"

"Sounds great. I'll be ready in five." Hailey walked over and gave Rob a hug, throwing her arms around his neck. "Thank you for bringing me. I really needed to get out of town. This is perfect." She smiled up at him. He had a bit of a five o'clock shadow, which made her catch her breath. Rob looked downright sexy just now. She pulled away and returned to her suitcase. She felt heat rising in her body. The same heat she had felt at the wedding. She cleared her throat. "The game will be fun tomorrow; I've never been to Wrigley." She turned to look at Rob, but he had left through the adjoining door to his own room.

They walked around downtown Chicago for about an hour. They went to Millennium Park and took pictures of each other in front of Cloud Gate, the big silver bean by Anish Kapoor. The weather was perfect for Chicago, low seventies, and low humidity. It was the spring between the harsh Chicago winter and the muggy summertime. They made their way back to the hotel, Rob said he needed to freshen up before heading to the hotel bar for his meeting.

Hailey was comfortable on her bed reading a book when Rob poked his head in.

"What are you reading?" he asked.

"A romance," she said, quickly putting the book down, she didn't want him to see the bare-chested man ravishing a debutant on the cover. "No judging."

"I wouldn't dream of it. I'm headed downstairs," he said.

She leaned up on her elbows. Rob looked downright hot. He was in a dark blue suit, a white dress shirt underneath with the top button undone. She nodded silently; words stuck in her throat. Finally, she was able to speak. "Go get 'em, you've got this." She smiled at him. Her heart was wanting to come out of her chest and that same heat was back.

Rob knocked on the door frame with his knuckles. "Knock on wood," he said. "I should be done within two hours or maybe even as little as two minutes if it doesn't go well." He looked at Hailey.

"Okay, well if anyone can do this, you can." She smiled at him and laid her head back down, picking her book back up. "Good luck, even though you don't need it," she called out as he slipped through the door. She closed her book and laid there with her eyes closed, enjoying the rush of endorphins she was experiencing. Ever since the wedding she'd been looking at Rob in a different light. A romantic one. She still couldn't figure out why, if he *was* feeling the same things she was feeling, why he hadn't ever said anything sooner? Or even given off a vibe or a hint? Why? He couldn't have been waiting for *her* to make a move, *could* he? Hailey was used to guys being assertive, taking what they wanted. She was used to men making the first move. If they didn't make a move, they weren't interested.

She'd always struggled with her self-confidence. Men paying attention to her was a sign that she, at least on the outside, was desirable. But the fact that so many relationships, not even relationships but connections, went nowhere, nagged at her that maybe the inside, her core, wasn't desirable. But her friendship with Rob made her feel like she, the real Hailey, *was* desirable. She just assumed he didn't find the outside of her...her looks, to be what he was looking for in a woman. Otherwise, he would have made a move by now. *Right?* This was the endless circular argument she'd been having with herself. She took a deep breath in. She felt a buzzing in her pocket. She fished the phone out. *That's weird, I thought my phone was in my purse.* She looked at the screen and realized she had Rob's phone.

MH: I'm almost there, sorry for the delay. The team's flight was late. See you in a few minutes.

Oh shit. Hailey had Rob's phone. She must have slipped it in her pocket after taking his picture in front of the bean... the one where Rob was pretending to hold it up. The memory made her smile. She jumped off the bed and slipped on her shoes, searched for her room key and ran down to the elevator to get the phone to Rob, hopefully before the player arrived. The elevator was taking its sweet time. *Finally*, she thought when it dinged with its arrival. She made her way down to the lobby and stopped at the concierge desk to get directions to the bar. She rushed as fast as she could without running. Stepping into the dark lounge, with its wood paneling and dark plush carpet, her eyes needed a moment to adjust. She spotted Rob in the corner. A man's back was facing her. She tried to wave to get Rob's attention, but he was so engrossed in handshakes and talking that he didn't see her.

She walked quickly over to the table. Her intention was to kind of just slide the phone to Rob and then leave as quickly and as silently as possible. She snuck up to the table, and quickly set the phone down, pushing it towards Rob with one finger. Rob's eyes caught hers and with a smile he acknowledged Hailey. She smiled back and turned around to stealthily slip away when she crashed into a server holding a tray with drinks. A loud crash rang out, and cocktails dripped off the front of Hailey.

"Oh my gosh, I'm so sorry," the server said while handing her a wad of cocktail napkins to blot the spilled drinks from her top.

"No, this was entirely my fault," Hailey replied.

"Here, let me help," she heard a deep voice say behind her.

She turned around and was face to face with *him*...#25. She felt her face flush as she looked into his dark hazel eyes which seemed to have more than a twinkle in them... more like a fire...a big, hot, roaring fire. "Uh, thanks," she croaked out.

"Hey, I know you," he said, as his mouth curved into a smile. He narrowed his eyes as he looked at Hailey, she could see the pieces fitting into place for him. He snapped his fingers. "I've got it...Phoenix Stadium...third base seats. You prevented your friend from getting smacked in the head with your good catch. Right?" His handsome eyes were dancing.

Hailey was practically speechless. How had he remembered *her*? She nodded her head up and down. "I think so?" It was all she could squeak out. She kept hearing a sound on her other side but didn't comprehend what it was until she turned and saw Rob.

"Are you okay?" His brows were knitted together as his eyes darted between her and Matt Harper. "Uh...Matt, this is my...err...friend Hailey. Hailey this is Matt Harper."

"I know," Hailey said as she kept nodding her head, a goofy grin spreading across her face.

Matt softly held Hailey's hand. "Nice to meet you, Hailey."

"I'm sorry to have interrupted your meeting. I'm going to go now." She looked again at the hunk of a third baseman, smiled and left, her face as red as a beet.

CHAPTER SEVEN

BLOCK THE PLATE: *A catcher who puts a foot, leg, or whole body between home plate and a runner attempting to score, is said to "block the plate."*

Rob was still processing what he had just witnessed. Hailey and Matt *knew* each other? It didn't seem they knew each other very well, something about a foul ball was the best he could make out. He shook his head, realizing that Matt was talking to him.

"So, your *friend*…Hailey…is she single?"

Rob looked at Matt who had a smile on his face and a glint in his eyes. He cleared his throat. *Shit, what do I say? Yes, she's technically single.*

"Because I'd love to get her number from you."

Crap. What to do? He had introduced Hailey as his friend… that was stupid, and she *is* single…but if he gives her number to Mr. Baseball she won't be single for long. But how can he stand in her way? He doesn't even know if she feels anything but friend feelings for him, his plan had been to talk to her tonight. But now he had this dilemma. Lie and say she's not single, find out tonight that she's not interested in Rob as any more than a friend and now he's ruined her chance at a relationship with a major league baseball player. A super handsome one. Or find out that she does like him more than a friend, but she would have liked Matt more...or if she ever found out that he blocked her chance with Matt she'd probably never forgive him. Rob swallowed hard and did what he did best, acted as a perfect friend *and* gentleman.

"She's single. But I want to clear it with her before I just hand her number out."

"Great, yeah, no problem," Matt replied.

"I've got to warn you though...she's off men right now," Rob blurted out.

Matt snorted. "Consider me warned." He picked up his drink a shook the ice.

"How do you know her?" Rob asked, he felt as if his throat was packed with cotton.

"I noticed her at a spring training game. She made a terrific catch on a foul ball that was headed right for her friend."

"And you *remember* that?" Rob was a bit incredulous.

"Shit, yeah. She's rocking that perfect combo of cute and sexy; I'm not going to forget someone like her." Matt smiled broadly at Rob.

Rob took a swallow of his drink. *Yep, not going to forget someone like Hailey.*

⌖

"Why didn't you tell me it was Matt Harper you were here to sign?" Hailey blurted out.

Rob had barely sat down before Hailey bombarded him. His meeting with Matt ran late so he texted Hailey to meet him at the restaurant and hold their table. It was the kind of in-demand spot that if you didn't show up within ten minutes they gave your table away. He took a soft garlic and rosemary roll from the breadbasket, tore a piece off and dipped it into the small dish of olive oil.

"I'm pretty sure I told you," he said in between bites.

"I'm certain I would have remembered," she replied. "I saw him at spring training, he's not someone you forget, that's for sure," she snorted.

He looked at her sitting across the white tablecloth from him. She took his breath away. Always. But tonight she looked especially beautiful. She was in the red dress, it had a deep v-neckline. A delicate gold necklace around her neck, her hair loose around her shoulders. This was supposed to be the night he came clean. Spilled his thoughts and feelings for her. But instead, he was knotted up about something else. *Someone* else. Matt Harper.

He hadn't said anything to Hailey yet about Matt wanting her number. He literally felt that he had an angel on one shoulder and Satan on the other. He'd been leaning towards his devil side during his walk to the restaurant. No reason to tell her, pretend that the exchange with Matt never happened. She'd never know.

But now, looking at her eyes brighter than he could remember them ever being as she went on and on about how great Matt was, what a great player he is, how hot he is, blah, blah blah, his angel side was taking over. He could feel his shoulders slump. How could he deny this opportunity to her? Wasn't he first and foremost supposed to be her friend? What kind of friend doesn't relay that a major league baseball player, who's certain to be a big star, and also happens to be tall and good looking wants their friend's phone number? Really? Ugh. What was he going to do?

"Rob…earth to Rob," Hailey said.

Rob snapped out of his thoughts. The server was standing at their table waiting.

"Rob, are you ready to order?" Hailey's eyebrows were raised, a look of confusion on her face.

"He wants your number," he blurted out.

Hailey looked at him as if he'd just sprouted a second head. "No, I'm pretty sure he wants my order. I'll have the tagliatelle with the lobster cream sauce, please." She smiled up at the server and handed him her menu.

Rob shook his head and waived the server away. "Matt wants your number."

Hailey looked at him, obviously not making the connection of what he was saying. Her brows scrunched down further. "What?" she asked as she took another bite of her bread. "Aren't you ready to order? I'm starved."

"Matt Harper. He wants your number." He leveled his focus at her.

She had a look of pure shock on her face followed by elation once she swallowed the mouthful of bread. Seriously, she looked like a kid on Christmas morning. A kid on Christmas morning who got everything on their list and then some. She was practically bouncing in her chair. Her face was winding up, but nothing was coming out. Yet.

3...2...1...

"Matt fucking Harper wants *my* number? Oh my God. Calm down Hailey," she said to herself as she began to fan her face with her napkin. "This isn't a prank, is it? Please tell me it isn't a prank, Rob, because I'll kill you if you're yanking my chain." Her face looked on the verge of disaster.

"No," he said quietly. "Not a prank."

"*Well?* You gave him my number, *right*? Oh my gosh, oh my gosh. Maybe he's called already." She began to dig furiously through her purse. It was a small bag so Rob wasn't sure how she could be having such difficulty finding her phone in it.

"No...I uh, wanted to ask you first. I'm not going to just hand out your phone number without checking it out with you first," he snorted. He took a bigger than normal drink of his wine.

"Not when it's freaking Matt Harper you don't need to check with me first!" She shrieked. Diners were looking her way. "Sorry," she said softly as she turned to look at several people nearby. Her face was pure glee. "Text it to him right now," she ordered, giddy as a schoolgirl, practically bouncing up and down in her chair.

"Now? Why don't we eat first, and then—"

"—*Eat*? I can't *eat* at a time like this! Hurry... hurry, text him my number!"

Rob reluctantly pulled his phone from the pocket of his jacket. He still wasn't sure that he'd done the right thing, because right now he felt as if he'd been slugged in the gut by a heavyweight champion boxer. Who *could* eat at a time like this? Not Rob.

"I thought you were 'quote' off men. What about that?" He was clinging to hope here.

"Not when it's a professional baseball player! Duh." She looked at him incredulously, giving her head a small shake. "Text him before he forgets who I am...he must be interested in a thousand women."

"Well, right. These guys have thousands of women Hailey, do you really—"

"C'mon Rob, hurry," she looked at him with pleading eyes as he texted Matt her number.

As it turned out, Rob did eat. He just couldn't remember anything about the evening other than the fact that Hailey was completely over the moon, starstruck, and ready to burst with joy over the idea of going on a date with one third baseman known as Matt Harper. Rob endured an entire evening of hearing every little detail on the guy Hailey could scrounge up on the Internet.

"*Born on July 5.* He's a Cancer!" Hailey excitedly announced. Rob wasn't sure what the import of that was.

"From Madison, Wisconsin…6' 5" 220 pounds…little sister going to University of Wisconsin on a volleyball scholarship…his favorite color is blue."

And on, and on, and on. And on.

Rob just nodded with each revelation; a fake smile plastered across his face as he drank way too much wine.

After they got off the hotel's elevator and neared their rooms, Hailey shrieked loud enough to be heard from the space station. "It's him!" She began waiving her cell phone around in the air while simultaneously jumping up and down.

"People are sleeping," Rob hissed at her. But she'd slipped into her room just as Rob heard her say "hello."

He'd like to say he was above trying to listen in on the conversation, but he had his ear to the wall after about two seconds of debating the pros and cons of such a move.

Two seconds later Hailey burst into his room.

"We have a date!" Her cheeks were flushed, and her eyes twinkled. "Tomorrow night, I assumed you'd be okay with that. I mean it's *Matt Harper!*"

"Yeah. Fine," Rob replied.

"I'm so excited! I'm going to need something new to wear. Let's go shopping tomorrow and you can help me find something." She spun around towards her room. "Gotta call Molly, she's never going to believe this." With that she shut the door to her room and was gone.

It seemed like everything had happened both in slow motion and in an instant. One minute he was planning a romantic evening with Hailey, determined to tell her he had feelings outside of the friend zone. The next minute? He's taking her shopping to find something to wear for her date with another guy. *How did this even happen?*

Through the wall he could hear Hailey's excited voice talking to her friend Molly. Every few minutes there would be a burst of giggles and a sudden shriek. She *was* excited about it. *Super* excited.

Rob flopped down on his bed. "I'm such an idiot," he said aloud.

CHAPTER EIGHT

B *ATTER UP: What the umpire says to start the inning.*
Hailey slowly opened her eyes and looked up at the ceiling. *Wait.* Did that really happen? Or was she dreaming that Matt Harper asked her out on a date? She sat up on her elbows and pinched herself. Nope. Not a dream! She could feel the warmth of pure excitement rise from her stomach like a balloon filling with helium. *Matt Harper!* Six feet and five inches of pure hunk. Professional baseball player hunk to be exact. She closed her eyes and smiled as she pictured his face. Dark blond hair, greenish coppery hazel eyes, square jaw, and that smile. *That smile!* She fell back onto her pillow and grinned from ear to ear. He was grade-A gorgeous. *And* a professional baseball player! How cool was that? Hailey loved baseball. And he wasn't *just* a professional player, he was on *her* team. The *Dodgers!* Things couldn't get any more perfect.

Quickly her mind went over the mental checklist of what she'd packed for this trip. Was anything suitable for tonight? Uh, probably not. She needed to get going so that she and Rob could go shopping for something new to wear. Matt had

50

said it was casual, but still, she needed to look *perfect*. She smiled as her mind traveled to Rob. What a great friend he is, she thought. How gallant and chivalrous it was for him to not just give out her number, although he totally could have to Matt freaking Harper. For him to clear it with her first? That was Rob to a tee. Mr. Dependable, Mr. Thoughtful, Mr. Perfect Gentleman.

She swung out of bed and made her way to the shower, taking a minute to daydream as she waited for the water to heat up. She thought about the look on Rob's face last night when she told him Matt had asked her out on a date. What was that look? If she didn't know better, she'd say that he had looked wistful, sad even. But that didn't make sense to her. They were friends. *Right?* She briefly thought back to the wedding they'd attended together. That feeling of something more. She shook her head and got her mind back into the present and stepped into the hot shower. She quickly got ready.

She knocked on Rob's door. They needed to grab some breakfast and then get a move on.

"Hey," she said when he pulled the door dividing their rooms open. Rob looked great. He was in jeans and a gray pullover, his tortoiseshell glasses perched on his nose.

"Look what I have," he said as he waived an envelope in front of her.

"What's that?" Hailey asked as she took the envelope from Rob's hand and pulled open the contents. "Two box seats to the game today?" The day was just getting better.

"Yeah, I guess they're from Matt. There isn't a note or anything. They're certainly better than the seats I bought. What time are you meeting him tonight?" Rob rubbed the back of his neck.

There's that look again, Hailey noticed. Rob's normally warm brown eyes looked flat. His entire demeanor was flat, maybe even a tad on the worried side. Like something bad had happened.

"Are you okay, Rob?" she asked, putting a hand on his shoulder.

"Fine," he replied, as he looked around his room.

"Because you don't look fine," Hailey said. She continued to watch him.

"Probably just hunger. I'm sure I'll feel fine after breakfast. I had a bit too much wine last night. That's all." He returned to his room. She could see him grab his room key, phone, and wallet. He put them in his pocket and walked back into her room.

"Okay, if you're sure," she said.

"Yep. Okay, so what's the plan today?" He smiled weakly at her.

Hailey's thoughts swiveled back to Matt and their date. "Let's grab a quick breakfast, do some super-fast shopping, toss the bags in the room and then head to the game. Matt said he'd come by here to pick me up around 7:30, which will give me plenty of time to shower and get ready."

※

Hailey still couldn't believe it. She was sitting across from arguably the most gorgeous man she'd ever laid eyes on. His eyes were the perfect blend of green, gold, and copper framed by thick lashes. She quite literally was losing herself in them. He had a perfectly chiseled jawline, the kind usually reserved for movie stars and models. He made her lose herself more than just a bit.

She and Rob had shopped that morning before the game. Hailey had decided on new, figure-hugging jeans and a white blouse cut low. For some reason Rob had kept showing her things that would have been more suited for an Amish celebration than a date with a major league baseball hunk. He stopped after she called him "Dad" for suggesting another boxy dress with a turtleneck.

"Hailey?"

"Oh, I'm sorry," Hailey said as she shook her head slightly. She gave him a big smile. She was so over the moon about being with Matt that she could hardly stay in the present. Honestly, it felt like an out of body experience. Her heart was racing, and her palms were sweaty. She needed to pull it together or this would be the one and only date with him. But why did her mind keep drifting to Rob?

"What did you ask me?" she said as she studied his lips. *Stay focused, Hailey! Such nice lips...*

"I was asking what you do for work." He gave her a wide smile. A heart stopping smile.

"I, uh, I'm a self-employed editor. I work with independent authors."

"Oh, okay. Do you like that? I mean, why do that instead of working for a publisher?" Matt asked.

"I love it. I get to work for myself from home which allows me to have a life. There's something to be said for being your own boss. It's perfect for me really and landing a good editing job for one of the main publishing houses is really difficult to do...so this works."

"Are independent authors any good?"

"They are, you'd be surprised. And many do quite well for themselves."

She tore off a small bit of bread and popped it into her mouth. "Do you like to read?" She looked at him, he was so damn hot she really needed to work on listening to what he was saying.

"Uh...I read Twitter." He laughed, his entire face lighting up.

"Oh…well…it *is* reading, I guess." She scrunched up her nose. "Audio books?"

"Nah, I don't listen to those, but I do listen to sports radio. Does that count?" He looked at her seriously.

"Uh, well, no but maybe they *should*?" she said.

"Had you always wanted to be an editor?" he asked.

"No. I thought I wanted to be a lawyer—"

"—God no," Matt said. He chuckled. "I mean first you have to do the whole law school thing and then that big test thing, and then you're a *lawyer*. Uh, no thanks." He held his hands up.

"Well, my friend Rob, *your* new agent, is a lawyer. He's a great guy."

"Yeah, I like him. I felt good about switching from Dan to him. Plus, I got to meet you." He gave her his million-dollar smile again. "So, why didn't you become a lawyer?"

Before Hailey could respond, the server came to take their order. Matt had chosen a steakhouse only a couple of blocks from the hotel where Hailey and Rob were staying.

"You're having fish at a steakhouse?" Matt said after they had ordered.

"That's not so unusual, is it?" Hailey said, her brows knitted down. "I mean, I ate a Chicago dog at the game today…I *am* a meat eater…I'm not anti-meat or anything crazy like that…I just thought fish might be a good idea for dinner." *I sound like an idiot.* "But I can imagine you need a lot of steak, you know…to keep up your strength and all." At that Hailey began to flush. "You were awesome today. Four for five with a walk and just a triple away from the cycle. Really great game."

"Thanks, yeah, I'm happy with it." Matt fiddled with his napkin. Hailey thought he even looked a bit shy talking about himself. She hadn't expected that.

"What made you want to be a big leaguer? Were you inspired by a favorite player?"

Matt laughed before responding. "To be honest, when I was in high school it seemed like a good way to get girls. And once the majors were in my sight I loved the idea of making a lot of dough doing something as fun as playing baseball." He nodded as he continued to eat his bread. He flashed her a big smile that made her stomach tickle.

It hadn't really been the answer she was expecting, but hey, at least the guy was being honest. "Well, that's cool. I mean, we all need to make money," she said. "Nothing wrong with that."

They continued their small talk through dinner and dessert. Matt walked her up to the door of her room.

"So. You know I want to see you again, right?" He looked into Hailey's eyes while he brushed a stray strand of hair from her cheek and tucked it behind her ear. Just that small movement moved the butterflies out of her stomach and replaced them with a stampede of elephants.

"You do?" she squeaked out. Her throat was dry. *He wanted to see her again!*

"I do," he said. He leaned down towards her. He took her chin in his hand and brought his lips lightly to hers. His lips were soft, and his breath was sweet from the after-dinner mint. A small sound escaped her lips. Matt's mouth curled into a small smile. He brought both of his hands to the small of Hailey's back and gently pulled her towards him. Her hands found his arms, her thumb running along the ridge of his bicep through his shirt. This time when he kissed her it was with more force. More intention. And it was good. Really good. His warm lips pressed against hers. His tongue found hers. Those elephants were running laps now, it felt like a full-on circus was happening there.

She brought her hands down the front of his chest. To say he had a six-pack would be an understatement, what he had felt more like a 12-pack. She leaned her head back and looked into his eyes. "What were you saying?" She smiled up at him.

"I was saying, I want to see you again. We're going back to LA in a week and a half for an eight-game home stand. I want to see you then. That is, if you want to see me too." He rubbed his hands up and down her back. He had spread his feet wider than his shoulders to bring his gaze closer to her 5' 5" level.

Hailey nodded her head. "I'd like that."

If someone had asked how she'd gotten back into her room, she would have said she'd floated in. She couldn't remember her feet touching the ground. All she could remember was the soft feel of his lips on hers and the hardness of his muscles under her touch.

CHAPTER NINE

S *ACRIFICE BUNT: A sacrifice bunt (also called a sacrifice hit or simply a "sacrifice") is the act of deliberately bunting the ball in a manner that allows a runner on base to advance to another base, while the batter is himself put out.*

"Fore!" Rob yelled out after Spencer shanked his tee shot. Badly. It ended up in another fairway.

Spencer turned around to face Rob. A look of incredulity on his face. Pure shock actually. He rubbed a hand over his face. "You *what?*" He shook his head as if he was trying to erase what he had just heard. "You're going to need to say that again, because it *sounded* like you said you gave Hailey's phone number to a major league baseball star. And excuse me if I'm wrong, but that would be like giving a coach passenger a first class ticket…no, not first class but a ticket to fly private. No disrespect, dude. But c'mon. The guy's a hunk, *I* think so and I'm not into dudes. I mean he's like fillet mignon instead of bologna. So. For the love of God, please tell me I misheard you." Spencer stared at Rob.

"Are you guys going to play or socialize?" An older, overweight man in loud golf pants yelled to them from his golf cart.

"Sorry, we're going," replied Rob as he got into their cart. Spencer shoved his club in his bag and slid in next to him. "I'll tell you what my thinking was if you stop comparing me to sub-standard luncheon meats," Rob said as he drove the cart to his ball.

"I'm all ears." Spencer motioned with one hand to continue.

"Okay. So, of course this wasn't the plan to have Matt Harper ask Hailey out. And *yes*, I know that as things stand now, I don't have a chance. But what was I going to do? The guy asked for her number. What would you have done?"

Spencer slid out of the golf cart and dropped a second ball onto the fairway. "Does that drop look fair to you?"

"Yeah, it's fine," Rob said.

"You wanna know what I would have done?" He took his shot, landing the ball five feet from the pin.

"Nice shot."

"Thanks," Spencer said. "I would have lied. Told him she already had a boyfriend. *You*."

"I had already introduced her as a friend," Rob said.

"Lie and tell him she already has *a* boyfriend. End of story."

"But then I would be denying Hailey a great opportunity. I mean, a major league baseball player was asking to take her out. How could I, as her friend, say no to that?"

Rob wished he could have said no. The trip had been hell for him after that. He had listened through the wall again to see whether Hailey was going to invite Matt into her room. He didn't think she would, but it was Matt freaking Harper, but she hadn't. She came into his room and gushed on for an hour about how awesome the guy was...down to how he liked his steak. How perfect he is, how they are going to go out again once Matt is back in Los Angeles. Then during the flight home she was on her iPad going through every single picture of him on the Internet, going back to his little league days. The four-hour flight felt like four days. That had been several days ago, and he'd been trying to dodge Hailey ever since. She finally got a hold of him that morning and asked to see him the next day. His plan of action was to tell her that most of these pro athletes were womanizers and couldn't be monogamous if their life depended on it. He hoped it worked.

"You could have easily said no. Haven't you ever heard the saying 'what you don't know won't kill you'? I mean, dude." Spencer shook his head.

"I want to win her heart fair and square," Rob said. "Not by keeping other guys away from her."

"Other guys? This isn't just another guy...he's a professional baseball stud." Spencer shook his head as he sunk his ball into the cup. "You're a better man than I am, that's all I can say."

CHAPTER TEN

HIT AND RUN: *An offensive tactic whereby a base-runner (usually on first base) starts running as if to steal and the batter is obligated to swing at the pitch to try to drive the ball behind the runner to right field.*

"Great hit, Daisy!" Hailey ran to the baseball lying in the grass, but not before Sandy had gotten to it and jumped up and down on his small front legs barking at it. "I've got it Sandy, good boy." The small dog walked off, his head up high. He laid down in the shade of the bleachers and waited for another evil baseball to chase.

Daisy Ruiz was the thirteen-year-old Hailey had been a big sister to for the past two years. Daisy's mom had died shortly after she was born. Her father had signed her up for a big sister so Daisy would have the "touch of a woman" as he had put it. Hailey had grown up without a mother or much of any female presence. Her mom had abandoned Hailey when she was seven years old. Leaving her with her emotionally distant and abusive father. Her father had often blamed Hailey for her mother leaving. Many nights he would come home from work and shut himself in his bedroom for the night. Leaving her to fend for herself. This was actually preferable to the times he was around. He criticized everything about her. Telling her she was stupid and ugly and a mistake in his life; going as far sometimes to say he wished she'd never been born.

Luckily, Hailey's grandparents on her mother's side had been in her life. Their loving influence had helped to counterbalance the lack of love and worse that Hailey had experienced. Their love had mitigated but hadn't fully erased the damage. Her grandparents knew that her father was harsh but hadn't known about the abuse. Like many kids in abusive homes, she'd kept it a secret, telling no one the shameful truth of what went on behind closed doors. She had been envious of her friends whose homes seemed happy and bright, filled with parents who were loving and supportive. She hadn't known what that was like, except for the time she spent with her grandparents. Her grandmother had passed when Hailey was ten. She had been devastated. But she came to be very close with her grandfather, spending countless weekends and summer vacations with him. Through him she had cultivated her love of baseball.

"Wow, you're on a tear today," Hailey said to Daisy as she watched Sandy dart from his spot under the bleachers towards the baseball rolling in the grass behind her. He was barking the entire time, as if the ball was a threat to humanity. "Let's take a break," Hailey called out to Daisy.

They sat on the grass, in the shade of a large tree. Sandy sat in Daisy's lap soaking up her attention.

"How's school going?" Hailey asked after taking a long drink of water.

"Okay, I guess. Lots of end of year activities. Lots to wrap up. I'm nervous about middle school ending and high school starting. Those kids look so much older than me." Daisy leaned back on one hand; the other was rubbing one of Sandy's ears.

"You'll be great," Hailey said. "You are so outgoing. I really admire how engaged you are with school activities. You'll do the same thing in high school and that'll be a lot of fun and you'll make a bunch of friends." She held out one of the oranges she'd brought as a snack. She studied Daisy's face; her brow was furrowed with worry. "Is it something else you're worried about?"

"Kind of…" Daisy took one of the oranges and slowly began to peel it.

"Boys?" Hailey asked with a smile. She watched as Daisy nodded her head up and down, chewing on her bottom lip.

"I just want to be myself; I don't want to be *Kardashianed*. But it seems like that's what guys like. Fake and made-up." She leaned down and kissed Sandy softly on his head. The dog responded by whipping his tail from side to side.

"Not all guys like that. You need to be yourself, Daisy. You're a great girl. You're smart, beautiful, athletic, and interesting. You are so full of brightness. You should never change who you are. Ever. Don't be like all those other girls that follow the herd. Be yourself." She put her arm around Daisy and gave her shoulders a squeeze and kissed her on the head. "Don't ever change who you are. You're perfect."

"Thank you," Daisy said as she looked at Hailey and gave her a smile. "I'm glad I have you to talk to." She looked at her phone. "I gotta go, my dad's here," she said. "I'll see you next week. Maybe you could help me with that English paper I was telling you about." Daisy looked up at Hailey as she turned to leave towards the waiting truck.

"Sure, I'd love to," Hailey replied while she gave a wave over to Daisy's father.

"Hi Mr. Ruiz," she called.

"Hi Hailey, thank you!"

At the same time Daisy was leaving, Rob was making his way towards Hailey. She had finally gotten ahold of him, and he agreed to meet her at the park.

"Hi Daisy," Rob yelled out, waiving.

"Hi Mr. Rob," Daisy replied with a big smile.

Rob smiled and shook his head.

Hailey smiled to herself. When Daisy first met Rob she would call him Mr. Steadman. He'd asked her to call him Rob, but her upbringing just wouldn't allow her to be so casual with an adult. So they had compromised on "Mr. Rob."

Sandy went berserk when he saw Rob. He raced up to him and began running in circles. Stopping to put his paws up on Rob's leg, his tiny shoestring tail moving so quickly it resembled a propeller on a plane. A complete blur. "Hey Sandy." Rob picked the little dog up and carried him towards Hailey.

"How'd it go?" he asked, nodding towards the equipment.

"Great, she's such a natural. I wish she'd go out for softball, but she says she's already got too many activities to keep up with. She's such a great kid," Hailey replied as she gathered the baseballs up. "You wanna go to the Thai place on San Vicente? They have that outdoor patio so Sandy can come with us." She looked over at him. He looked good as always in shorts and a t-shirt from a surf shop in Malibu.

"Sure," Rob replied. "Did you guys walk here?" He picked up the bag of baseball equipment and slung it over his shoulder.

Hailey nodded yes as they walked to Rob's car. He put the bag in his trunk.

Once they were settled at the restaurant, they ordered their food. The server brought a dish of water for Sandy who made himself comfortable under Hailey's chair.

"So why have you been avoiding me?" Hailey asked as she took a sip of her bubble tea.

"I haven't been avoiding you, I've been busy. I had to make a trip out to Palm Desert to sign a minor leaguer. I've been busy with work, that's all." He looked at the label on his beer bottle, peeling a corner off with his thumbnail.

"Okay. Well, it's been weird how quiet you've been since we got back from Chicago. I thought maybe you were mad about the whole 'Matt' thing." She used her fingers for air quotes.

"Why would I be mad about that?" He looked up at her.

Hailey shrugged her shoulders. She took a stab at what had been her gut reaction to Rob's silence. That somehow, he was jealous. That had been her intuition, but her head told her it couldn't be that. They were friends. If Rob had those kinds of feelings for her he would have said something by now. But something about his avoidance of her since they'd returned was making her wonder.

"I wanted to know if you want to go to the game Friday? Matt gave me two front row seats next to third base." She smiled before taking another sip of her drink. The thought of Matt only made her smile these days. They'd talked and texted every day while he was on the road. After Chicago, the team had gone up to Milwaukee to play the Brewers. Matt had been tearing the cover off the ball lately. He was on fire.

They had grabbed a quick dinner together late last night once the team was back in town. Her entire body had lit up when she laid her eyes on him again. The dinner had been very romantic, white tablecloths, candlelight and a sumptuous Italian dinner which had been difficult for Matt since he was avoiding carbs. During their meal Hailey had half-jokingly said something about him having a different woman in every state to have dinner with and she was his SoCal hookup. She was surprised and thrilled when he'd reached for her hand and told her she was the only person he was currently dating and that's how he rolled. After dinner he'd driven her back to her apartment and had kissed her goodnight. She asked if he wanted to come in...she'd *really* wanted him to, but he'd declined, saying he had to be up early to meet with his trainer. She couldn't wait to see him again.

"Sure, sounds good," Rob replied nodding his head. He took a long drink of beer from the bottle. "Are you two going out afterwards?" His gaze and thumb went back to the semi-destroyed label.

"No, he said it's too late after the game. But they're playing a day game Saturday, so we're going out that night." Hailey was beyond excited...hopefully he didn't have any early morning obligations Sunday, because her body was currently on code red as far as needing something beyond just kissing. She and Molly had gone out shopping and made sure Hailey was prepared for just about any occasion from going to the gym to a black tie affair and everything in between. She had all her bases covered, even down to new bras and underwear. Molly had insisted that she needed these to change her dating luck, telling her she should probably sacrifice the old stuff by burning it. Hailey had reluctantly gone along with it despite the extra hit to her bank account.

The server brought their food, and they were quiet as they dined on the pad see ew and panang chicken curry. They made some small talk about the Dodgers, Rob had spoken about nearly every player except Matt, Hailey noticed. Afterwards, Rob drove her and Sandy home.

"See you Friday," she'd called out to him and waved goodbye as she watched him drive off. She scooped Sandy up under one arm. "What's going on with him?" she asked the small dog. Sandy let out a big snort in reply.

CHAPTER ELEVEN

W*arning Track: The dirt and finely ground gravel area along the fence, intended to help prevent fielders from running into it.*

Rob and Hailey headed to Dodger Stadium. Hailey wanted to get there as soon as the gates opened so she could lay eyes on Matt as often and as much as possible. Rob reluctantly agreed. Since they wouldn't have time to grab food on the way, they settled for a couple of Dodger dogs and beers.

After watching batting practice, they made their way to the seats. Rob had noticed that the smile hadn't left Hailey's face since Matt had waved over to her. They were sitting in the front row next to third base. Hailey would be able to keep an eye on Matt all night. *Fantastic.*

He took a drink of his beer before putting it back in the cup holder and looked over at Hailey. She had never been a "high maintenance" type of woman but tonight she was more done up than she would normally be for a baseball game. She looked good. *Really good.* She was in form fitting jeans, and a white tank top, Dodger blue Converses on her feet. Her hair was done in soft waves that framed her beautiful eyes. The pink gloss on her lips was incredibly inviting. Rob hoped the hot dogs and beer would wipe it off so that he could stop focusing on them. Her usual vanilla and orange scent was all around her. It was intoxicating.

"I'm entirely happy to eat hot dogs and beer for dinner anytime," she said as she popped the last bite of bun into her mouth, washing it down with a drink of cold beer. She took a napkin and wiped it across her lips.

"Agreed." Rob wiped his hands with some napkins, thankful the pink gloss was now gone.

The players were streaming onto the field to begin their warmups. A combination of stretches and movements to loosen them up for the game.

"There he is," Hailey bubbled. She was digging in her purse, emerging with a tube of lip gloss in one hand.

Rob glanced over as she reapplied it to her lips.

"How does it look?" she asked as she pressed her lips together in a kiss.

He swallowed hard. Cleared his throat. "Good, I guess."

Hailey barely listened. She had 1001% of her focus on Matt. Watching him do a variety of muscle stretches. Rob was pretty sure he heard her say "oh my God" ever so softly when Matt had bent down, his back to them, feet shoulder width apart, forearms touching the ground. *This is torture.* He looked up at the cloudless sky. This was one time when he was wishing for a rain out.

From Rob's left a southern accent wafted through the air. "Excuse me, oh my I'm so sorry, I didn't mean to step on your little bitty toes."

He turned to look. Coming to sit next to them, no not sit, but stand with her hands on the low wall in between the seats and the field was a woman with big strawberry blond hair. Like really big. She had on a white figure-hugging dress with her assets spilling out the front. Her high heels were cherry red.

"Excuse me, sugar," she said to Rob. She practically purred. "But which one is Matt Harper?" She had a deep southern drawl and was pointing to the field.

By now Hailey had noticed this woman and was slowly appraising her, looking her outfit up and down through narrowed eyes. "That one," she said as she pointed to Matt. "The one with the jersey that says *Harper*," she said sarcastically.

"Why thank you. I have this little bitty ball I'd like him to sign." She began to waive wildly in Matt's direction. "You hoo, Matty, would you do me a tiny favor?"

Matt noticed her right away, nearly every man on the field had. She was hard to miss. He came jogging over with a big smile. Once he got close he gave Hailey a wink. At least it looked like it was for Hailey. Rob glanced over at her; the smile was gone.

"What can I do for you?" Matt asked the Georgia peach. His eyes were taking in the *entire* package.

"Would you sign this ball for my nephew? It would make him happier than a tick on a hound dog. He's back in Decatur and hasn't been well." She bent over the wall, if she leaned any further one of her breasts was apt to just fall out of her dress.

"Sure thing," Matt said with a wink that was without a doubt for the curvaceous woman. He handed it to her before running back onto the field.

"He's *taken*, you know," Hailey said, her arms crossed in front of her chest.

The woman turned back towards them and looked Hailey in the eye. "Sugar, they're *never* taken." With that she turned and left.

"Did you hear that?" Hailey let out a puff of air. "I can't belief she was so...so *forward*! Matt would certainly not be taken by all of that, would he?" She motioned around her breasts with her hands. She turned her focus to Rob.

"Uh..." He ran a hand over his face.

"She's gotta a lot of nerve," Hailey huffed. "And what a ridiculous outfit to wear to a baseball game. Unbelievable." Storm clouds remained on Hailey's face. This was what Rob was afraid of. Baseball players attracted women better than picnics attracted ants. Especially baseball players who looked like Matt.

"Groupies," Rob said. "You saw Bull Durham. Groupies." He shrugged his shoulders. "Kinda goes with the territory, Hailey."

"The territory! What?" She turned towards him. Fear mixed with confusion were in her eyes. "Bull Durham is a movie, not real life. Right?" She searched his eyes.

"Gosh Hailey, I don't know what to say. Art imitates life. Isn't that the saying? Pro athletes do attract women. Lots of them. You know that. Why would you think Matt would be any different?" He didn't want to hurt her but on the other hand, he needed her to know the truth. She needed to know what she was facing.

"I just...I just didn't get those kinds of vibes from him. It was just me and him at dinner. Just Matt. Not baseball star Matt." Her shoulders slunk down. The glee that had been on her face earlier was gone. Long gone.

"Maybe just talk to him," Rob said encouragingly. "Have a conversation and see how he reacts to your concerns." She seemed to brighten a bit at that.

"Okay," she murmured.

Just then the announcer came over the loudspeaker and began to introduce the players. By the time they said Matt's name, Hailey seemed to have put some of her concerns behind her. She jumped up and down and screamed and clapped when Matt's name came over the PA system.

The rest of the game went well. Hailey seemed happy and Rob was actually able to put the whole Matt issue on a shelf and enjoy a night of baseball. The Boys in Blue won, and Matt had a good game going three for four and making an incredible defensive play to save the game.

❦

Rob watched the bubbles in his beer rise to the top of the glass. He absentmindedly rubbed his thumb against the condensation that had formed on the mug. He was waiting for Spencer at their favorite sports bar, but his thoughts were 100% on Hailey and her date with Matt.

"Hey, sorry I'm late." Spencer slid into the booth across from him. "I have a bad feeling about this," he said as he flagged a server down.

Rob looked up at him. "Yeah, me too. I know the three-date rule and this is only, technically date number two, but they've been talking on the phone and they saw each other at the game last night, so I think the three date thing is out the window. She'll probably end up in his bed tonight." He picked up his mug of beer and drained it in one gulp.

"Date? I was talking about the Lakers tonight. I have a bad feeling that they're going to lose. What are you talking ab—" Spencer rubbed a hand over his beard. "Shit, tonight's *the* date."

Rob relayed to his friend the incident with the woman at the baseball game and how he'd tried to talk to Hailey about the reputation for skirt chasing pro athletes had.

"How'd she take it?" Spencer asked before dragging a French fry through some ketchup.

"She was surprisingly naive about the whole thing. It's as

if in her mind, Matt Harper can do no wrong. She really didn't see him as that type of guy." Rob pulled the bun from his hamburger, slathered some mustard on it before placing it back on. He wiped his hands with a napkin. "I mean, I can't really believe this guy is so different from most athletes, can you?" He looked at Spencer before biting into his burger.

"No, he's probably not different. He's probably a dog like the rest of them. He's young, good looking—"

"Yup," Rob said.

"—he's on the Dodgers and he's got women like this southern gal throwing themselves at him." Spencer grabbed a few more fries from his plate. "I mean, what did this chick say? 'They're never taken'? Sounds like she knows what she's talking about."

Rob took a deep breath. "Yeah." Suddenly he wasn't hungry anymore.

"What's wrong? This should be good news for you. The sooner she finds out that he's a low down rotten scoundrel, the sooner you can get back to your plan of telling her how you feel." Spencer put his hand up to get their server's attention. "You want another?" He nodded at Rob's empty beer mug.

"Sure."

Rob sat for a minute, sorting out the conflicting feelings he was experiencing. On one hand, Spencer was right. The quicker Hailey found out that Matt, *maybe*, was a womanizer with someone in every town, the sooner she would possibly be his. *Maybe*. Other than the moment they shared at the wedding, there had never been any kind of vibe from Hailey saying "hey, I might like you as more than a friend." Never. But he'd never find out if he didn't ask. And he wouldn't be able to ask while she was dating Matt. The other possibility was that Matt *wasn't* like the other sports stars. Part of him hoped he wasn't. He didn't want to see Hailey get hurt, no matter what he stood to gain from it. Maybe this thing with Matt was going to work for her. And she'd be happy. The thought of a happy Hailey made Rob feel good. More than anything, he wanted her to be happy. Even if it wasn't with him. But he sure did hope he would get his chance to be the one who would make her happy. Because the image of her spending her life with someone else felt like a gut punch. The kind you didn't see coming.

CHAPTER TWELVE

LEFT ON BASE: *A base runner is said to have been left on base or stranded when the half-inning ends and he has not scored or been put out.*

Hailey studied her reflection in the mirror and liked what she saw. She should, it had taken her three hours to get ready. She wanted to look perfect for her date with Matt. After she got home last night, she'd called Molly and relayed the whole incident with the southern floozy. Molly had calmed her nerves and pointed to the fact that Matt was dating her and if he was interested in floozies or groupies then he'd be going out with them instead of Hailey. This had made perfect sense and had calmed her enough so that she was able to sleep.

Her thoughts were interrupted by a light knocking on her door. *It's him!*

She took a deep breath, studied her reflection one last time and went to the door, pulling it open. And there he stood. Pure gorgeous perfection. He was in dark jeans and a white button-down shirt with the sleeves rolled up, revealing very tan and very, *very* muscular forearms. Hailey's mouth went dry. In her opinion, forearms were an underappreciated part of the male anatomy.

"Hi gorgeous," he said as he leaned in to kiss her cheek. "You smell as beautiful as you look." He handed her a bouquet of soft pink roses he'd had behind his back.

"Thank you," she managed to squeak out. "C'mon in while I put them in water." She pulled the door open wider, closing it behind him.

"And I mean it. You look gorgeous." He looked her up and down in a way that made her stomach go all flim flammy. After trying on at least a dozen outfits, she'd settled on a white cotton dress with tan strappy sandals and lots of turquoise jewelry that she'd picked up during her many trips to Scottsdale.

"Thank you, you look gorgeous too," she replied. "Just make yourself comfortable while I put these in water," she called out.

"I like your place," he said.

She'd only been gone from the room for a second when she heard Sandy making a huge commotion. She dashed into the living room to see what the problem was. Matt was sitting back on the couch and Sandy was next to him, but instead of being his normal sweet self, Sandy had decided that this was a stranger-danger situation and was growling and barking viciously at Matt, the hair on his back standing on end.

"Sandy, what's gotten into you. Quiet!" Hailey said to the small dog.

"Yeah Sandy, what's gotten into you. Usually women like me," Matt said as he turned and winked at Hailey.

"Sandy's a boy," Hailey said slowly, a note of disappointment in her voice.

"A boy?" Matt looked completely confused. "But her name's Sandy."

"*His* name is Sandy. You know…like the pitcher."

Matt's face looked as blank as a new chalkboard.

"Sandy Koufax?" she said, her eyebrows raised.

Finally a light bulb went off in Matt's head. He pointed a finger gun at Hailey, "gotcha." He stood up and brushed his pants off. "It's fine. I'm not a big dog person anyways."

Hailey hardly heard him as she raced to the kitchen and hastily put the flowers in a vase of water. She wanted to get Matt away from Sandy before the dog decided to take his free bite.

Matt drove them to Santa Monica where they dined at Wolfgang Puck's Chinois, a delicious Asian and French fusion restaurant. They were seated in a quiet corner and started with the house special lychee martinis.

"You probably know more about me than I do about you, with Wikipedia and all," Matt said as he bit into a lobster egg roll. "God, these are good," he said before Hailey could answer.

"Oh my, they *are* good," she said as she let out a small groan.

"Just what I like, a woman who enjoys her food, hard to find around here." He waggled his eyebrows at her. "So, did you grow up in LA?"

"I did. I've been here all my life, including college. I went to UCLA. Kind of dull I guess." She looked at him. He was clean shaven and smelled like leather and blackberries.

"Not dull. I would have given my right arm to have escaped the brutal Wisconsin winters growing up. I was elated when the Dodgers drafted me. I hope I never end up living in a cold climate again," he said, shaking his head.

They chatted some more as they dined on the famous chicken salad, duck fried rice, and moo shoo pork.

"So, what's the deal with Sandy? Does he hate all men?" Matt asked as they were sharing a pear and yuzu custard dessert.

"No, it's weird. He doesn't. He loves Rob," she said, wiping her mouth with a napkin.

"Hmm," Matt replied. "I was certain you and Rob were an item even though he'd introduced you as a friend. I wanted to make sure before I asked for your number, but he assured me, said you two were just friends."

Hailey felt irked for some reason. *Just friends.* She was upset at herself for allowing her imagination to think that there had been something more than 'just friends' happening between her and Rob after the wedding. But there it was in black and white. *Just friends.*

"Yeah, we are. I'm finished, are you ready to go? That was a delicious dinner, but I think I need to get up and walk a bit now." She smiled at him. How could she even be thinking about Rob when she had this gorgeous hunk on her arm?

They walked along the shops of downtown Santa Monica. The moon was full, and the weather was a perfect 75 degrees. Matt had gotten more than a few stares. Even if people didn't know he was a Los Angeles Dodger, it wasn't every day that you saw 6'5" of near male perfection.

"My place is close by if you wanna go. We could sit on my balcony and watch the ocean." He had placed her small hand in his very large one.

She nodded, "I'd like that."

They made their way to his car and within minutes had pulled up in front of a group of condos fronting the beach. Matt unlocked the door and stood back to allow Hailey to enter first. "It's not much, I had to find something fast when I got called up."

Hailey knew that Matt was making the league minimum salary of $500,000 which was a lot of money, but not in Los

Angeles. The place he was renting was small and modest but had a balcony with a beautiful view of the ocean. The night's moon was shining its silvery beam across the water.

Matt handed her a glass of wine and sat down next to her on the outdoor sofa. He sat back, put his arm around her and rested his legs up on the ottoman that also served as a coffee table.

"This is nice," Hailey said, she took a sip of the cold, crisp wine. Matt's warm arm around her shoulders, his leg against her leg. The sound of the ocean could be heard when the waves crashed ashore.

"Thanks. I like it a lot. Not too far from the stadium and I get to be at the beach. I'm making up for all those cold winters." He laughed.

Hailey couldn't stop thinking about his leg against hers. Or the hard muscles she'd felt back in Chicago when they'd shared a kiss. She could feel her cheeks begin to flush just thinking about that kiss.

As if he'd read her mind, Matt turned towards her. He took the glass of wine from her hand and set it down before he took her cheek in one hand, cradling her face. His eyes made contact with her eyes and then they trailed down to her lips. He brushed his thumb along her mouth and then brought his lips to hers. Hailey moaned with pleasure. His lips were hands down the softest she'd ever felt. She wrapped one of her arms around his shoulder, sliding her hand down his arm, feeling his biceps through his shirt's fabric. She wanted to just rip the shirt from his body. This was not like Hailey, she usually let men come to her, but this guy was whipping her hormones up into a soufflé.

They continued to kiss. Matt gently brought his tongue to hers. Hailey's core was now officially on fire. She was like molten lava inside and she was ready to erupt. She started to unbutton his shirt just a bit, rubbing her hand along his chest. It was just as magnificent as she'd imagined. His skin was smooth, the muscles hard. Rock hard.

"You feel good," she whispered into his ear. She heard him let out a moan of his own. He began to kiss her neck and her throat. Hailey was wearing a shirt dress that had buttons from top to bottom. She was just waiting for Matt to begin unbuttoning them as they continued to kiss. He made his way up to her ear, nibbling the lobe. Hailey's breathing became shallower. She was dying for more.

Matt brought his lips back up to hers, using his tongue. He eventually stopped and kissed her on the top of her nose. Well, that didn't feel very sexy, she thought.

"We need to stop," he said as he buttoned his shirt back up. He stood up and held out his hand to take hers. Hailey could tell from the front of his pants that his body hadn't gotten the message that the party was over.

"You mean, stop out here and go inside?" she said. *Maybe that's what he means.*

He let out a bit of a laugh. "No, I mean we need to stop for the night." He must have noticed the confused look on her face because he immediately offered up an explanation. "Trust me, I want nothing more. And I mean *nothing* more than to take you into my room, undress you and lay you on my bed."

Hailey was nodding her head enthusiastically as Matt went through the steps he'd like to take with her.

"But?" she said.

"Well, you know how superstitious ball players are, I'm 30 for 42 with five home runs and 12 RBIs in my last nine games. No sex for the time being." He looked at her, his hands on his hips. "Nope, not going to happen. Not as long as I'm hot. We're stuck on first base for the time being."

CHAPTER THIRTEEN

HOME FIELD ADVANTAGE: *Teams playing home games have a small advantage over visiting teams.*

"No way, no how. I'm not representing the guy. Period." Rob glared at Jonathan Chin, a junior partner at the firm.

"But Rob, Devin specifically asked for you to represent him." Jonathan took a seat in the chair in front of Rob. He picked up a pencil and began to lightly tap it on the desk.

"I don't care. Let someone else sign him. I don't represent abusers. Period. That's why I stick a clause in my contracts stating that if anyone is involved in domestic violence, any kind of hate speech including homophobic slurs, racist slurs or actions, or misogynistic words or actions they are immediately dropped as a client."

"*Alleged* domestic violence in this case," Jonathan replied.

"There are pictures of her face and an eye witness, Johnathan. It's hard to imagine it's anything other than what it appears to be. If someone else wants to sign him, be my guest." Rob leveled his eyes at the other attorney.

"You're not going to make partner by refusing to take clients," Jonathan said as he got up from the chair and straightened his tie.

"If refusing to represent creeps prevents me from being partner, then so be it." Rob returned his attention to a stack of papers on his desk.

Jonathan shook his head as he left Rob's office.

He heard his phone vibrate. Caller ID showed it was Hailey. Great. Now he gets to hear about how great Mr. Baseball was last night.

"Hey, Hailey," he said, trying to force a smile into his voice.

"Hi Rob, can you do me a big favor and watch Sandy tomorrow? I hate to ask you on a workday."

"No problem. I'm in the office all day, I'd love to dog sit."

"Great! Tomorrow's an off day for the team so Matt and I are going to hang out at the beach."

"But Sandy loves the beach, why aren't you taking him?" Something that felt like hope was rising in Rob's chest.

"Matt and Sandy didn't really get off on the right foot, I guess he's not a big dog person," Hailey said, her voice had just a touch of melancholy to it as she said this.

But this was great news for Rob. Dogs were *everything* to Hailey, if this guy wasn't into dogs then it couldn't last long.

"Wow. I thought you said that anyone who didn't like dogs must be a psychopath."

"I didn't say he didn't *like* dogs. He's just not a dog nut, like you and I are. Of course he's not a psychopath Rob. Jeez."

"Okay, okay. I'm just repeating what you said to me."

"Let's not get into it okay? Just drop it." Hailey sounded irritated. "Thank you for taking Sandy," she said, her voice a bit softer.

"No problem. I love spending time with him."

After getting off the phone Rob pondered this new information. He didn't get why Hailey didn't seem concerned about the dog issue. Normally she would never go to the beach without Sandy. *Normally*. He guessed things must be far from normal.

❧

"Wow. He must have mind control powers, like Killgrave and Professor X," Spencer said as he shoveled some loaded nachos into his mouth.

Rob and Spencer were at one of the many great taquerias in the city. Rob had just relayed to his friend how shocked he was by the whole dog issue. Normally Hailey would have given a guy the boot if he didn't like dogs.

"Comic book characters? Really?" Rob had a pained expression on his face as he looked across the table at Spencer.

"I don't mean *he's* a comic book villain. I'm just saying it's like he's got that kind of hold over her. He's bamboozled her with his baseball star status. And the fact that he's a stud. Just saying…it's got Hailey not thinking clearly." Spencer popped another chip into his mouth.

"Yeah, he does seem to have her not thinking straight." Rob mussed as he sat quietly, nursing his beer. He was still in shock that Hailey was giving Matt the time of day, to be honest. Dogs were a huge part of who she was. She loved dogs. All dogs. Shit, if something had a dog on it, she *bought* it. Hailey going to the beach without Sandy was *way* out of character for her.

"Maybe it's the sex?" Spencer visibly cringed when he said this. "I hate to bring it up, man. But maybe this guy is a rock star stud in bed."

"Nope. They haven't slept together." Hailey had relayed all the details to him. He hadn't wanted to hear any of it, but much to his relief she had told him about being stuck on first base. At least he didn't have to push from his mind, images of them together in bed.

"Really?" Spencer's eyebrows raised as he bit into his carne asada taco.

"Yeah. The guy's been on an unbelievable hitting streak. He's superstitious like most athletes are and doesn't want to have sex. He's afraid it will mess up his batting. And not just sex, but anything beyond kissing he won't do."

"Huh. Yeah, I saw he had two home runs last night, right? His bat *is* hot. At least the other bat isn't hot too." Spencer kind of chuckled to himself, digging into some guacamole before he noticed Rob's expression. "Sorry, man. But hey, gotta take the victories where you can find them." Spencer shrugged his shoulders before waiving for the server to come to their table. "What happens if he stays hot?" Spencer asked, shoving a chip loaded with guac into his mouth.

This question caught Rob off-guard. What *would* happen if Matt's bat stayed hot? How long could Hailey go out with this guy with nothing more than kissing going on? Was it possible that this could tank everything? Rob didn't think so but it was something to hope for. Rob wasn't a religious man, but he was going to pray that Matt Harper's bat continued to be hot.

For the next 10 days Rob heard very little from Hailey. The team was still in town and he could only guess that she was spending all of her extra time with Matt. He missed spending time with her. Matt would soon be out of town though for an eight-game road trip. Perhaps then he could spend some time with her.

Rob: Hey, how's it going?

He was surprised when she texted him back right away.

Hailey: Great. Sorry I've been MIA. Matt's heading out on the road tonight. We'll be able to catch up after that.

Rob: How about the beach on Wednesday?

Hailey: Don't you have to work???

Rob: I have worked a lot of weekends this year, I'm due a weekday off.

Hailey: Sounds great! I'll work hard to catch up with my writers so that I can have a relaxed day. Sandy too?

Rob: Of course. You don't even have to ask.

Rob couldn't wait for Wednesday to come around.

❦

"Robbie, sweetheart, come in." His grandmother pulled him by his hand and planted a kiss on his cheek.

"Grandma is that another new perfume?" he asked.

"It is. This one is Valentino. Doesn't it smell heavenly?" she asked as she led him into the living room.

"It does, you never cease to amaze me." Rob walked into his grandparents' living room. Their house was a Spanish-style two story in Los Feliz. His grandpa was sitting in his chair, folding up and setting a newspaper down on the ottoman in front of him.

"Hey there Rob, so good to see you," his grandfather said as he got up with the help of a cane.

"Don't get up for me grandpa. How's your new hip?"

"Oh, it's fine. I feel like a new man." His grandfather smiled warmly at him, his eyes crinkling around the corners. "We should head into the dining room anyhow; you know how your grandmother gets upset if we're not ready to eat when dinner is ready to be eaten." He gave a wink over to Rob.

"I heard that," called his grandma from the kitchen.

"The old bird still has good hearing," his grandpa said in a low voice.

"I heard that too," his grandma said as she came into the dining room. Her hands full with plates of food.

Rob walked over to her. "Here grandma, let me take those," he took one of the dishes from her hands. "What else can I bring out from the kitchen," he asked.

"Just the bowl of salad, dear," she said to him. "How's Hailey?"

"Okay, I guess. I haven't talked to her much lately," he replied, putting the large wooden bowl of green salad down on the table.

"Is she still seeing that ballplayer?" she asked.

"She is," Rob said. "He's gone for the next eight days for road games. I'm taking her and Sandy to the beach Wednesday." He sat down and passed the bowl to his grandfather next to him.

"Good, you can make your move," his grandmother said. Her eyes dancing with mischief.

"Grandma, I'm not going to make a move on Hailey while she's seeing someone else. That wouldn't be right." Rob helped himself to some rice and salmon.

"Pfft. What's 'right' is for you and Hailey to get together. That's what's right. I had Miss Milly do a reading for you yesterday. And—"

"A fortune teller?" Rob's eyes were wide. "Grandma, I can't believe you believe in those things."

"Oh shush. Miss Milly is good, she's from Barbados and she's got the connection, I'm telling you. While she was doing a reading for you the 'lovers card' turned up—"

"Of course it did," Rob said quietly. He looked over at his grandfather who was trying to keep a smile from spreading over his face.

"Now Robert, are you going to let me finish or not?" She gave him a stern look.

"Sorry Grandma," a chastised Rob replied.

"The lovers card turned up and gave you a twin flame spread." She looked triumphantly at Rob.

"What does that mean? That my love life is going up in flames?"

"No. It means that Hailey is your true love and that the baseball hunk will be out of the picture soon. If you play your cards right." With that she forked a piece of salmon into her mouth.

Rob thought about this. It seemed like a bunch of nonsense. But one thing that wasn't nonsense was that he did need to play his cards right. Hailey was the one for him. The only one. Somehow Matt needed to be out of the picture. The sooner the better. If Miss Milly turned out to be correct, then Rob would instantly be a believer.

CHAPTER FOURTEEN

HOOK FOUL: *When the batter pulls the ball down the line, starting fair but ending foul.*

Hailey had on shorts and a t-shirt over her bikini, a new Dodgers cap from Matt, and sunglasses. Sandy was on her lap, his nose sticking out the window as they sped down the Pacific Coast Highway. The overcast sky was beginning to break up, making way for the bright blue hiding behind them.

She looked at Rob and smiled inside. He looked good in sunglasses and white t-shirt. His window was down, and the wind was ruffling his soft brown hair. She felt that familiar tickle in her chest when she looked at him. They had spent countless days at the beach together over the years. Sometimes they rented bicycles to ride on the path that went from Venice Beach to Pacific Palisades, Sandy tucked into the basket on Hailey's handlebars, stopping to eat at one of the many places on the beach to grab something casual. She and

Rob had shared a lot of fun times together. Hailey felt a small tug on her heart.

By the time they were on the beach with chairs out and the umbrella up, the sun was shining brightly. The sound of the ocean waves pounding the shore was only interrupted by the sound of the gulls overhead. They sat together as they watched Sandy run along the beach as fast as his little legs would carry him. He came to a screeching halt at the line where the water met the sand, let out a few barks and then turned and ran back towards them.

"He loves the beach so much. It wasn't nearly as enjoyable without him last week," Hailey said. She scratched the dog behind the ears before he took off running for the water again.

"But you had Matt, your new lap dog." Rob had a smirk on his face as he rubbed sunblock on his legs.

"Ha ha," Hailey replied, before sticking her tongue out at him.

"I was kind of shocked that you didn't take him," Rob said, looking at her. She glanced away and got busy burying her toes in the warm white sand.

"Yeah, well…wasn't my idea. Matt really talked me into it just being the two of us. It was fun. Just different without Sandy," her voice was wistful. She had been upset that Matt hadn't wanted Sandy to come with them. But in the end, he'd made it out to be a romantic day out together and that it would be so much more fun with just the two of them, telling her that the restaurant he planned on taking her to didn't allow dogs and it would be too much of a hassle to drive Sandy back home first. The fact that he wasn't a big fan of dogs did niggle at Hailey a bit. It probably should be bothering her more, but she figured in time he'd come around to her dog. She hoped.

"How *are* things going with him?" Rob asked. He pulled a water bottle from the cooler and offered it to Hailey.

"It's going good," she said, taking the chilled bottle from his hands.

"He gave me this." She held her wrist out to him. On it dangled a delicate silver bracelet from which an enameled baseball charm hung. She turned the charm so that Rob could see the back side. #25 was engraved on the back.

"Oh," Rob said. He swallowed hard.

"Yeah, it caught me by surprise, it's really very sweet of him. And he *is* sweet." Her gaze was focused on Sandy. The little dog was barking at the ocean. Getting the bracelet had caught her completely off guard. They were enjoying a romantic dinner at a seafood restaurant in Malibu with a sweeping view of the ocean and the setting sun. Matt had handed her the small box wrapped with a burgundy ribbon. She had immediately felt the familiar pit in her insides. The one she got whenever she was given a gift. The experience always took her right back to being a little girl. As a child Hailey had dreaded getting presents and any holiday in which she would be getting gifts. Her father would often accuse her of "not looking happy enough" while she unwrapped the present. He would snatch it from her and tell her she didn't deserve anything, before sending her to her room. His voice booming through the house, followed by the slamming of his bedroom door. It didn't matter if it was Christmas or her birthday, the same scene had played out multiple times. It became a self-fulfilling event. Her dad would see the fear created by him on her face whenever she had a gift to open and he'd react to it. She hadn't been a good enough actress to pull off a different expression despite trying her best.

Having people around whenever she had gifts to open wasn't any better. She could feel her dad's eyes on her. She would detect the slightest hint of disapproval on his face. A look that was so subtle, it went undetected by those around her. It was her own private hell. Once they were home, he would take the gift from her, telling her she didn't deserve it. He often asked her, "why can't you be like the other kids?" At the time it didn't occur to her young self that the reason she wasn't "like the other kids," was because she had an abusive father. At the time she thought it was *her*. She thought she wasn't good enough and that she was intrinsically bad, after all even her mom had left her. Years of therapy was beginning to chip away at the damage. The memory of this pain was always stirred up whenever she was given a gift. She realized, as an adult, that what she had gone through wasn't normal and had been very damaging. She told herself she deserved gifts, just like everyone else. But it didn't *fully* prevent the pit from starting to form in her stomach or her body from beginning to tense up whenever she was handed a gift to open. She gazed out at the ocean and swallowed hard, shoving the feelings back down before it brought tears to her eyes.

"You don't seem entirely thrilled," Rob said. He took a long drink of water.

"I, I am. I just..." she let out of big sigh. "Now that he's been gone a few days I've been able to mull over things. All my therapy and meditation have allowed me to step back from situations better than I used to be able to. It allows me to reflect."

She tried to finish her thought without revealing too much about her relationship with gifts. She'd never fully opened up to Rob about her past. Only hinted at it.

"Sandy, no!" Hailey yelled as she suddenly sprung from her chair and ran towards a couple on the beach. Her little dachshund was sitting in the middle of their blanket, back on his hind legs with his small front feet up in the air, clearly begging for some food. Hailey scooped him up, apologizing to the young couple and brought him back to their spot. "He nearly scored a sandwich. They thought he was so adorable."

Sandy looked up at them with his dark brown eyes.

"As his attorney, I must say that this dog is innocent of all charges," Rob said. A huge smile broke out over his face as he watched her break into laughter.

"Well, in that case, maybe a small treat is in order," she said.

Sandy seemed to know what was going down and sat back on his haunches, paws raised up in the air in classic beg-mode, while Rob fed him some bits of cheese from the cooler.

They relaxed in the sun, had lunch, and played some Frisbee together. Sandy wore himself out running after the hovering disc. By the end of the day all three of them were exhausted.

"Better get going, I've got some paperwork at home needing my time since I was gone all day," Rob said as he stood up, taking up one end of the blanket spread out before them.

Hailey instinctively grabbed the other end and they shook out the sand together. "Okay, thanks for taking us. It was great spending the day together, I've missed spending time with you." She looked at Rob.

"Same," Rob had replied.

She never finished telling Rob what she was feeling about Matt, and he had left the subject alone.

❦

"Hey handsome," Hailey said into her phone screen. Matt's chiseled face lifted her spirits a bit. "How's New York?"

"Cold and lonely without you babe. I hate travel days."

The team would be facing the Mets for four games and then on to Atlanta for three before wrapping up the road trip with three games in Miami.

"It must be exhausting flying and living out of a suitcase." Hailey looked into Matt's eyes.

"Sure is. And with the time difference it's brutal. What did you do all day beautiful?"

Hailey beamed. "We went to the beach with Rob. Just spent the whole day hanging out and relaxing…catching up."

"We?" Matt's eyebrows lifted just a bit.

"Me and Sandy. I felt bad that he'd missed the beach when you and I went."

"He's a dog, Hailey. He doesn't miss anything. Except food. He'd probably miss that, but that's about all." Matt chuckled and shook his head.

Matt's dismissiveness of Sandy wasn't sitting well with Hailey. But she pushed it to the side. She was trying to tell herself it wasn't anything to be alarmed at. Matt's attributes far outweighed this one flaw. At least she hoped so.

"What kind of swimsuit did you wear. I hope it wasn't a bikini…Rob would be drooling all over you." Matt became serious.

"Well…yeah, it was a bikini…and no, he wasn't drooling, he's seen me in a bikini before…we're friends…remember?" Hailey didn't like this possessive vibe she was seeing. She'd wear whatever she wanted to thank you very much.

"Sorry babe. I just don't want anyone else looking at the goods. Even if he is 'just a friend.'" Matt used air quotes.

Before Hailey could weigh in, Matt continued. "You look great in your bikini. Man, you are exactly what I dreamed California girls looked like when I was suffering through the endless Wisconsin winters. Blond, tan, athletic and shapely at the same time." He let out a low whistle.

Hailey felt herself blush. "Stop it. You're embarrassing me

now. Not to mention you're making me wish you were here. How are we going to get through the next 10 days?" She looked at him, her eyes hooded.

"It will go by before you know it. You know the rules though. As long as I'm hitting, we're sticking to first base." He looked expectantly at her.

"I know. First base. Got it." She let out a strangled laugh, before letting out a big sigh through pursed lips.

"Gotta go, babe. My room service is here."

"Okay, good luck tomorrow…I'll be watching!"

After they disconnected, Hailey thought back over the conversation. While she was talking to Matt or when she was with him, she couldn't sort out her thoughts, she often would drift back over the spoken words later when she was alone. She didn't like the reminder that he wasn't into dogs, and she certainly didn't like the streak of jealousy and possessiveness she'd gotten a peak at. But maybe these were good things. If Matt was the womanizer Rob suggested he might be, would he then be jealous of other guys seeing her in a bikini? Would he be possessive if he had women everywhere? Hailey didn't think so. He'd be too busy to worry about her. Not to mention that he wouldn't be doing anything as long as he was batting like an all-star. What was he going to do? Go to first base with other women? That didn't make sense to Hailey, and this thought made her feel more comfortable and settled. She came to the conclusion that Matt's behavior was proof positive that he was a one-woman man.

CHAPTER FIFTEEN

I NTERFERENCE: *An infraction where a person illegally changes the course of play from what is expected.*

"So, how's it going, Hailey?"

Hailey looked at Dr. Boone. She was in her usual "uniform" of slim pants, a crew neck cashmere sweater, and a silk scarf tied elegantly around her neck. Hailey had been coming weekly to the Brentwood office located in a beautiful Spanish-style bungalow for the past two years.

"It's going okay," Hailey responded.

"Just okay?" Dr. Boone peered at her over the top of her reading glasses.

"I mean, good. I guess." She chewed on her bottom lip. She still got anxious when talking about her feelings. It was never easy.

"Last we talked you were on cloud nine with Matt. What has changed?"

Hailey squirmed in her seat. "I mean...things...nothing

has changed. To be honest, I'm not sure *how* I feel. I should be feeling great."

"Should?" Dr. Boone raised her eyebrows.

"I know…I'm not supposed to be driven by *should*." She made air quotes.

Dr. Boone nodded in agreement but remained quiet.

"I just don't understand why I'm not feeling over the moon about him still."

"What were the attributes that made you feel 'over the moon' about him?" Dr. Boone crossed her legs at the ankles.

"He's a major league baseball player for starters. He's incredibly handsome…I mean catch your breath kind of handsome. And…" Hailey trailed off. What else had she been attracted to? Was this it? Baseball player and hot? She sat quietly while she searched her brain. Several minutes passed.

"Let's try this," Dr. Boone said. "Before you met Matt you had been focused on your friend Rob. You'd had an epiphany at the wedding you attended with him and felt that there was something more there that would come out in the open soon…despite my suggestion that you take some time off from relationships to explore yourself. What is it about Rob that you think would make a good partner for you?"

Hailey couldn't help it. She broke out into a broad smile at just the mention of Rob's name. "Well, for starters, he's sweet, handsome, loves baseball, works in the baseball industry, loves to read, loves dogs…especially Sandy, is close with his family…he's got a really great family." She took a breath. "He always seems to know what I need and is always there for me. We have fun together. I feel like I can relax and be myself with him." She looked down at her hands in her lap.

"That's quite a list," Dr. Boone responded. A small, uncharacteristic smile on her lips.

Hailey remained silent.

"So, why are you dating Matt and not Rob?"

"I...well...Matt just kind of showed up, and he made it clear he was interested. Rob has never made a move." She examined her fingernails.

"Aren't some of those items on your list signs that he might be interested in something more than friends?"

"I mean...wouldn't he have..." Hailey trailed off. Were these signs that Rob was interested? Was it possible he was acting above and beyond just a friend? Molly was a friend, yet as much as Hailey loved Molly there was a different feel to the closeness in her relationship with Rob.

Silence filled the small office for several minutes.

"Let's pivot from Rob. What are your plans for your relationship with Matt?"

"I'm just waiting for him to return from the road trip and then we'll pick up where we left off. Except where we left off was exactly nowhere."

"Yes, you mentioned at our last session that he wasn't willing to go beyond kissing as long as he was hitting well. How do you feel about that?" Dr. Boone tucked a gray hair behind her ear.

"I'm not sure. I mean, in one way it's kind of nice because I won't be even more blinded by adding sex to the mix. It's heady enough that he's a pro-athlete and super handsome. No sex allows me to look at the rest of the relationship. But I'm also worried. How long will this last? What if he hits well all year?"

"In the past you've mentioned that sex was a way for you to feel, albeit temporarily, validated and desired. Can you feel those things with Matt without sex?"

Could she? "I think so. I mean, he could go out with anyone and he's going out with *me*." Hailey looked hopefully at Dr. Boone.

"Let me ask you this. Do you feel validated by Rob?

Likable? Desired?" Her eyebrows were raised as she waited for Hailey to respond.

Hailey had never considered this question. "I do," she said. The realization hit her like a ton of bricks.

"How does that make you feel?"

"Good…except…I can see where you're going with this."

"Oh? And where is that?" Dr. Boone asked.

"You're trying to make a case for a relationship with Rob. But the problem is that I don't think he feels that way about me no matter how many nice things he does for me or how well we get along. He's a nice guy…he would do this for anyone."

"Except he's chosen *you* to do it for."

And it was this comment by Dr. Boone that hung with Hailey all day. *He's chosen to be this way for me.* Hailey knew that Rob had his good friend Spencer and many other friends, but none were female and none were as close to him as she was. She honestly couldn't see him wiping vomit from Spencer's face. But then there was Matt. She was still hanging on to this being something good. She was certain he would come around to Sandy and that they would find other common ground. Even if they didn't, maybe there was enough there to build on? Only time would tell and she couldn't wait for him to come back to Los Angeles so they could pick up where they'd left off.

☙

"I've missed you so much," Hailey said. She looked at the small screen of her phone. Matt's face, with a day's worth of stubble, stared back at her.

"Same," he replied as he ran a hand through his hair, a tight smile on his face.

Hailey wrinkled up her nose and furrowed her brows.

"You know, everyone has a bad night or two. It doesn't mean anything. Just part of the cycle. You can't stay hot forever."

Matt had gone one for five the night before and today he'd been zero for five. "Babe, I'm batting in double digits the last couple of days."

"That's why they call it an average...yours will be just fine. You'll be hitting again, don't worry about it." Except worry was practically spelled out across his face. And while Matt certainly wasn't happy about his batting slump, Hailey was secretly delighted. It would finally mean they could get beyond first base! She just had to get through a few more games and then Matt and the team would be home. Hailey was counting on rounding the bases with him.

"But what if I don't? What if the streak was just luck?" He rubbed a hand across his face.

"You didn't get into the majors by being lucky. You got there because you're good. Damn good. You need to look at the bigger picture or you're going to make yourself crazy."

"Maybe. I really need something to change my luck up." He ran a hand over his face.

"Wish I was there to be your rabbit's foot." Hailey could feel her cheeks warm.

"My *what*?" He narrowed his eyes, his face blank.

"You know...your lucky rabbit's foot." She looked at his face, total confusion covering it. "Didn't you ever have a rabbit's foot key chain when you were a kid?"

"Uh...no. I can't even picture that. What was it made from?"

Hailey's face scrunched up. *Is this guy for real?* "A rabbit's foot."

A look of disgust washed over his face. "A real rabbit's foot? Babe, that's gross."

"Maybe it's not a Wisconsin thing. I got one as a kid at the flea market. It was pink." Now that she thought about it, it did sound kind of weird and a bit morbid but was the kind of thing that you didn't question as a kid.

"Never mind about the rabbit's foot...I wish I could be there to be your good luck charm, if you know what I mean." She let a small smile escape. "Maybe I could change your luck."

"Definitely. But we'll have to wait until I get back. Hey, I gotta go, my room service is here." Matt's face lightened at the mention of his meal.

"Okay, good luck...break a leg! Rob and I will be watching you guys destroy the Mets this weekend." She gave him her biggest smile...a little encouragement never hurt anyone.

"Thanks babe." With that, the screen went black.

As it turned out, it was the Dodgers that got destroyed and Matt went one for fourteen over the series. No walks and certainly no home runs. The hot streak was officially over.

CHAPTER SIXTEEN

JAM: *To pitch far enough inside that the batter is unable to extend while swinging. "The pitcher jammed the batter."*

As soon as Rob knocked on the door he heard Sandy's customary *someone's at the door* barking frenzy. The noise was so loud he could barely make out Hailey's voice yelling that the door was unlocked and for him to come in. *Unlocked? That's not safe.* But he forgot about any safety concerns as soon as he stepped into her normally tidy apartment, he went slack jawed from shock.

There were stacks of bowls, pots, and containers on every single flat surface of her apartment. The air had the acrid smell of burnt food. *Really* burnt food. Several fans were oscillating, and all the windows were open. Hailey was wearing an apron covered in so many food stains that it was nearly impossible to tell what the original color had been. And speaking of Hailey...she had her hair back in a ponytail, several strands of hair were glued by perspiration to her forehead, and her eyes looked half wild.

Rob looked down at Sandy who was giving him a look as if to say, "I'm glad you're here for the intervention." And an intervention would not have been out of the question because Hailey didn't cook. As in ever. The only things she cooked were boxes of mac and cheese and sandwiches.

"What's going on?" he asked as he surveyed the damage.

"Matt comes home tonight and I thought I'd surprise him with a whole bunch of pre-made 'Matt-approved' meals," she replied.

Except it didn't come out like normal human speech but rather as if she were an audio book set at double speed.

Rob closed his eyes for a moment and rubbed his temple. "I don't even know where to begin." He looked up at Hailey. "First, how much caffeine have you had today?"

"I don't know. I just started on a second pot of coffee."

"Second *pot?*"

She was nodding her head quickly in agreement. "What's your next question?" Her eyebrows raised as she wiped some sweat off her brow with her forearm.

"What exactly does 'Matt-approved' mean?" *Did the guy give her a list of likes and dislikes?*

"You know...protein forward, lots of veggies, no additives, no sugar, paleo style eating, lots of zoodles."

"Zoodles?"

Hailey held up a piece of zucchini that resembled a slinky. "You know, noodles made out of zucchini."

"Okay," he said slowly. "I'm pretty sure that's not a real noodle."

"Right, because it's a zoodle."

"But you don't cook, so...*why?*"

She turned her back to him and resumed cutting up what looked like chicken. "He's been in such a slump I know he's going to be in a bit of a funk. Since he's been on the road for ten days his fridge will be empty and I want to take care of him by stocking it up with all kinds of healthy foods. I can finally put all these take out containers I've been hoarding to good use." She nodded her head to a tower of black, rectangle shaped plastic food containers.

"Okay...a couple more questions," he said as he bravely tried what looked like a dish with sweet potatoes and chicken. "Wow, this is actually good," he said with surprise. "How'd you learn to do all this?"

"YouTube mostly. I'm glad you like it." She dumped the cut chicken into a skillet. "It's been all trial and error. It started out mostly error, that's why it's smoky in here. But after a couple of bad batches, I think I've got the hang of it." She turned and smiled at him.

"I didn't know you were seeing him tonight. What time does the team get back?" Rob's eyes roamed the various food boxes filled with different foods.

"About nine. I was going to wait until about 10:30, once I know he's most likely home and run this all over to him."

"Wait. Doesn't he know that you're coming over?" Rob stopped eating and wiped his hands on a nearby towel.

"Nope. I thought I would surprise him." She beamed a big smile at Rob.

Rob grabbed a beer from the refrigerator. "Want one?" He looked over at Hailey, holding out the cold brown bottle.

"Nope, I'm good. Need to stay alert and awake for tonight."

Alert and awake? "Whoa...wait...this isn't just about food, is it." It was said as a statement, not a question. Rob was starting to get a rock-like feeling in his stomach and it wasn't from the zoodle he'd tried.

"Maybe not," Hailey replied slyly. Her face shaded just a bit pink before she busied herself with some more chopping.

Of course, Rob thought. Matt's major league slump would mean that he no longer was being superstitious about sex and there was no more reason to stay on first base. The realization hit like a ton of bricks. Acid began to back up into his throat. "Maybe surprising him isn't the best course of action here," he suggested hopefully. "Maybe you should call him and plan when to come over." *Maybe if I'm lucky, Matt will get back on a hitting streak before Hailey can see him.*

"Nope. Don't agree. Even if he's tired, I can just give him the food and leave. No reason why he needs a heads up to accept a delivery of healthy food." She transferred some of the cooked chicken into another to-go box before sticking the skillet onto the heap of dishes already overflowing in the sink.

"I don't know, Hailey. Don't you think it's too early in the relationship for surprise visits? You don't know what kind of mood he'll be in, or what his routine is whenever he returns home from being on the road. Wouldn't it be better to call first?" He plopped down on her couch and took a long drink from the bottle of beer. Sandy pranced up his set of stairs leading to the couch and sat next to him, resting his head on Rob's leg, and raising one eyebrow as if he too was interested in Hailey's answer.

"I don't understand why you keep insisting that I call first." Hailey's voice contained just a touch of irritation. "I mean really. Why on earth could he possibly be upset about me bringing over a whole bunch of food to fill his refrigerator with? Why?" She popped a piece of melon into her mouth and shook her head. "Not everyone is as formal as you are Rob." She shook her head and began to work on the mountain of dishes.

Rob mulled over how to reply and eventually decided that this was one of those times when maybe he shouldn't. So, he just stayed quiet. He went into the kitchen and grabbed a clean dish towel. "I'll dry," he said.

Hailey turned to him and smiled. "Thank you."

❦

Rob drove down Wilshire Boulevard to his house. The top down, the scent of oleander and oranges scented the air. It was one of those Los Angeles evenings that made him happy he'd splurged on a convertible. But as he drove, he felt a lump form in his throat as he thought about how much effort Hailey had put in to pleasing Matt.

Rob wasn't exaggerating when he said that Hailey couldn't boil water. She struggled with grilled cheese. But somehow, she'd practically transformed herself into Martha Stewart. She must have spent hours watching YouTube videos and meticulously shopping for all the ingredients needed for the recipes. *For Matt.* The lump that had formed traveled down from his throat to his chest and lodged there like a rock in the sole of running shoes. He was overwhelmed with a certain ugly feeling. Jealousy.

This was the longest he'd ever seen her stick with one guy. He'd never had to watch her doing things for another man before. Ever. And he didn't like it. Watching her excitement and energy all poured into doing something to take care of Matt felt about as much fun as a root canal, without Novocain. Something he would sign up for in a heartbeat if it meant she could be his. If she was cooking for *him* and not Matt.

It hurt and worried him. She'd only been going out with Matt for about a month now and already she was doing things for him that she'd never done for Rob. That was the hurt. It made him feel as if he wasn't as important as the third baseman in her life. The other emotion was worry. He was worried about losing her. Losing her as a friend and more. As long as she was in this relationship with Matt there would be no opportunity for Rob. He only hoped he could hang on to his friend status. He swallowed hard and snapped on the radio. He needed something to wrestle his thoughts away from Hailey.

"Well, I can say this...our guys in blue didn't look good the last half of the road trip and we can only hope that playing at home will improve things.

You are 100% right Gene. The second half of that road trip was abysmal. You didn't mention the elephant in the room but I'm going to. Matt Harper. That was not the look of a professional ball player. He couldn't get his bat on the ball if his life depended on it. I can honestly say I don't think I've ever seen an uglier stretch by someone who had been so hot. He needs to do something to change his luck. Baseball players are notoriously superstitious creatures, so whatever activity he's been doing or avoiding needs to change immediately."

"Shit, shit, shit!" Rob swore aloud and his hand smacked the steering wheel. Hailey was going to be the reason for Matt's change in luck. Probably starting tonight. She was the proverbial lamb before the slaughter except in this case the lamb was running to the butcher. He felt as if he was going to be sick.

CHAPTER SEVENTEEN

T OSSED: *When a player or manager is ordered by an umpire to leave a game, that player or manager is said to have been "tossed."*

Hailey was on cloud nine as she made her way to Matt's place in Santa Monica. The inside of her car smelled heavenly from all the food she'd prepared for him. *Tonight is the night!* As bad as she felt over his hitting slump, she couldn't be happier over the actual fact that they would be moving past first base. *Finally!* She had on her sexiest bra and panty set. Yes, she might be jinxing things by making some assumptions here, but there was no way in hell she was going to be caught in a ratty bra, or even worse: granny panties. Nope.

Hope and excitement mixed within her creating near euphoria. No more hot bat meant no more sexually frustrated Hailey. She moaned aloud at the mere thought of stripping clothes off Matt's hot body. Just the thought of seeing him naked caused her to press her thighs together.

She stepped on the gas. Second, third, and home bases couldn't come fast enough. Yes sir, she would be rounding the bases tonight.

She pulled up in front of his unit and gathered the bags from the back seat of the car. She could hardly keep a lid on her excitement. But she reminded herself that she needed to be mindful that as happy of an occasion this was for her, Matt was probably not going to see it as 'happy.' He had to be incredibly distressed over his batting slump. She needed to tread lightly. She needed to use the right amount of concern and empathy before ripping clothing from his body and throwing herself at him.

She made her way up to his front door, set the bags down, and rang the bell. Anticipation bubbled over her like champagne spilling from its bottle. She could hardly stand still.

"Just a minute," she heard him call out.

When the door opened Hailey wasn't ready for what she was about to see. Matt wearing only a towel, wrapped loosely around his waist. *Sweet baby Jesus.* Her eyes roamed slowly over his body. His chest and shoulders were pure perfection. And his stomach. The word chiseled came to mind as she took in his abs. She had to close her jaw before drool began to spill from it like a cartoon character. Her eyes made their way up to his. And his expression was one of surprise mixed with what looked like panic. She could hear him talking to her through her daze.

"What?" she asked, trying to focus on the words coming out of his mouth.

"What are you doing here?"

"I, um, I missed you." She smiled.

"You should have called," he said in a clipped tone as he looked back over his shoulder. One hand on the door.

Okay...not the reaction I was hoping for. "I know. I wanted to surprise you. I figured you wouldn't be feeling the best and would be coming home to an empty kitchen, so I made you some paleo meals." She held up one of the bags. "I wanted to do what I could to take care of you." She smiled hopefully at him.

"You really should—" Matt squirmed and tightened the towel around his waist.

Just then Hailey heard a woman's voice calling out. "Are you coming back?"

Panic began to seep into her chest. She stood up on her tiptoes and peered over Matt's arm to see a tall, leggy redhead wearing only one of his jerseys standing in the hallway.

Her stomach dropped; her eyes darted to Matt's. "What's going on?" she asked, her eyebrows furrowed, her cheeks beginning to heat up in anger.

Matt just shrugged his shoulders. "You've seen the way I've been hitting. I needed to shake things up." He cracked a small smile.

"Shake things up?" Hailey said incredulously. "You could have shaken things up with *me*!" She shook her head. "Why her?"

"Ginger's been there for me before. I knew I could count on her to rustle me out of my slump. I told you I'm superstitious about these things, it's nothing personal babe."

"Then why have me around?" Hailey said in an agitated voice. "I don't get it. I thought you were into me...why were you even dating me?"

"Hailey. Babe. You're a knockout...you've got the whole girl next door vibe going on. You're the type of girl I bring to press events and family gatherings."

"Hey!" Ginger apparently was taking issue with not being good enough to meet the folks.

"Sorry babe." He shrugged his shoulders as he turned his

head back towards Ginger. "You got a bracelet, what more do you want?" he said, more as a statement than a question.

Hailey's mouth dropped open. "She got a bracelet too? What...do you buy them by the hundreds?" Her heart raced while disappointment made its way to the pit of her stomach and gripped it. Her hand made its way to the bracelet on her right wrist. She touched the baseball charm with her fingers.

"Of course not. That would cost a fortune, babe. *Hundreds.*" He snorted. "I only bought a dozen...I got a discount that way."

Hailey stared at him in disbelief. Without thinking and with one fluid motion she yanked the bracelet off her wrist and dropped it at her feet. "Oh, and here's something else for you." She picked up the container of chicken and zoodles with homemade marinara sauce and channeled her inner Sandy Koufax, winding her arm back before pitching it forward and releasing the container towards Matt's chest. A lump of red and green with white chunks of chicken slid down his body.

"Hailey, can't we talk about this? C'mon babe, be reasonable."

"Reasonable? Why couldn't I have been what turned your luck around? Had it ever occurred to you that the one you get lucky with and the one you bring home to mom and dad could be the same person?"

"Ginger's always turned my luck around...I wasn't taking any chances." Matt snorted, "But she's definitely not the type you bring home...she's more the bedroom type, if you get my meaning." He winked at Hailey as he said this.

"I'm leaving!" came Ginger's voice from the house.

"But we're not finished!" Matt called out over his shoulder. "I need to fix this."

"Then call a chiropractor...I don't need to be disrespected like this. I have feelings too you know."

"Uh, could you leave the bracelet then? I'm down to my last two. I can give you a signed bat instead. Cool?"

Hailey let out a mirthless laugh and turned to walk off. While she had her back to him, she heard Matt yell out after her.

"That's right...go back to your quote *friend* Rob," he snorted.

Hailey spun around on her heel. "What did you say?"

"Your friend...Rob. He's got a monster crush on you. I'm pretty sure you can go running into his arms for some comfort."

Hailey stood blinking. "What makes you say that?" She had a funny feeling in her stomach. What did it feel like? She wasn't sure. Tickly...somersault like.

"It's the way he talks about you. The way he looks at you. It's pretty obvious. He's in love with you."

Well, it hadn't been obvious to Hailey. She tumbled the idea around in her head to see if it made sense. Did it?

She looked up to see Matt wipe a finger through the sauce that remained stuck to his chest and put it in his mouth. "Mmm. This is good. Hey Ginge...let's talk. Also, can you cook?" he called over his shoulder before shutting the door.

Hailey made her way to her car and slid behind the wheel, softly closing the door. She sat for a minute. She didn't turn the engine on yet. Matt's words were bouncing around in her head like popcorn being popped. *He's got a monster crush on you. He's in love with you.*

Could this be true? She thought about the look she'd seen in his eyes while they danced at the wedding together. And about the electricity she'd felt when they'd touched. Was it possible that Rob was feeling the same things about her as she felt about him? Her mind wandered back to Chicago. Rob had said he wanted to talk to her about something while they were there, but now that she thought about it, they hadn't talked. But why?

And then it came to her...Matt. She had met Matt before Rob had a chance to talk to her. That had happened before they had dinner together that first night at the romantic and beautiful Italian restaurant. Her cheeks flooded hot at the thought. Now it made sense...the look on Rob's face when he'd relayed that Matt wanted her number. Her chest tightened at the memory. She felt horrible for being so oblivious...for being so caught up in the idea of Matt Harper being interested in her. It hadn't dawned on her that Rob might have been hurting over the whole idea of it.

But wait...*had* he been hurting? If his plan in Chicago had been to tell her he wanted to be more than friends, then why had he asked her about giving her number to Matt? Wouldn't he have just told Matt she was taken? She shook her head as she turned the engine on. She was confused and until she knew for certain what Rob was or was not feeling, she certainly wasn't going to ruin things by asking. Especially not now. Not as it was beginning to sink in what had just happened. Her heart squeezed at the reality that Matt was a typical professional athlete, not immune to women throwing themselves at him. Not only was he not immune but he also took them up on their offers. Wholeheartedly.

"Jerk," she said aloud as she headed back to her apartment. Rob had warned her, and she hadn't listened to him. She'd been so convinced that somehow Matt was different. Her heart sank. No, she wasn't willing to look the other way to be in a relationship with a baseball player. Especially not *this* baseball player. He didn't even like dogs for Pete's sake. He didn't read. And he seemed to have gone into baseball for un-pure reasons as far as she was concerned. Money and women. He'd said it himself. What an idiot she was.

She called Rob as she grew closer to her apartment.

"Hailey," he said as he answered. "Are you okay? Aren't you at Matt's place?" She could hear pure concern in his voice. *He's just a friend, Hailey.*

"Change of plans. Wanna meet at my place and take an Uber to Jalisco's for some tequila and tacos? Emphasis on the tequila." There was a pause of silence.

"Of course. I'll meet you at your place," Rob said quietly.

That's what good friends did. They could tell when something was wrong and quietly agreed to be there for you. She certainly wasn't going to mess with that no matter what Matt had said about Rob. *"He's in love with you."*

CHAPTER EIGHTEEN

DESIGNATED FOR ASSIGNMENT: *A process that allows a player to be removed from his team's 40-man roster.*

Rob sat down after getting off the phone with Hailey. *What happened at Matt's?* He could tell by the tone of her voice not to ask questions. And the fact that Hailey mentioned tequila was a huge neon Vegas-style sign saying something had gone wrong. Really wrong. Hailey was not a big drinker, and when she did drink it was beer, wine, or maybe a margarita type drink. She certainly wasn't the type of girl to start slinging shots. He ran through some scenarios in his head as he got ready to leave. He knew she'd talk to him when she was ready.

And then, like a breaker being thrown when circuits were overloaded, his emotions turned to anger. *What had Matt done to her?* Something had happened. The thought of Matt hurting Hailey in any way made Rob clench his fists. It made him want to smash the guy right in the face. Wait...who was he fooling? Harper would pulverize him in a minute. But it would be worth it, he thought as he grabbed his keys and headed to Hailey's apartment.

Hailey hadn't said anything during the Uber over to Jalisco's. Nor did she say much before ordering Patron shots along with tacos and nachos.

"I think I might stick to beer; I've got work tomorrow." Rob waived a hand for the server to come back to their corner table located at the back of the restaurant. It was quiet since it was Sunday evening. Mariachi music wafted from the speakers and the brightly colored interior of yellow and turquoise lent to a festive environment.

Hailey pointed a finger at him. "You introduced me to him so you're drinking shots with me."

The expression on her face was hard for him to read. Did she seem upset? Not particularly. She seemed pissed off. Rob sighed in resignation before throwing back the small glass of the clear liquid. It burned his throat as he took a bite of the lime wedge the server had placed on their table. Hailey's blond hair framed her face. He watched as she tucked a piece behind her ear. She looked him in the eye.

"Okay, I think I'm ready to talk about it."

She spent the next fifteen minutes rehashing what had occurred when she'd shown up unannounced at Matt's house. "I know you had said to call first and to not show up unannounced, but it's a good thing I did. Otherwise I wouldn't have found out about his little side piece keeping him company. Ginger. Or 'Ginge' as he called her," she said, mocking Matt's voice with a little shake of her head. "You tried to warn me about professional athletes. I was just too stupid to listen." She scooped up an enormous nacho and ate it in one bite.

"You're not stupid, Hailey. Just because a lot of pro athletes womanize and aren't monogamous, doesn't mean they all are that way. I'd hoped he was one of the good guys too." He flagged the server down for a beer and two waters.

"And two more shots," piped up Hailey.

Rob raised his eyebrows at her. "Is that a good idea?"

"I don't have to work tomorrow, so you can go ahead and have your beer...I'm sticking with the shots." She gave him a small smile.

"*Shots*...plural?"

"Maybe...don't be a dad right now, Rob."

They ate a couple of tacos while they sat in silence.

"You were hoping Matt was one of the good guys?" Hailey put up air quotes.

"I was." He took a drink of beer.

"Why?" She eyed him, brows furrowed.

"*Why*? What do you mean *why*?" Where was she going with this?

"Why would you be rooting for Matt to be one of the good guys...it sounds like you were hoping it worked out between us." She studied him, her eyes a bit glassy from the tequila.

Rob swallowed and wiped his mouth with the napkin in his lap. "Because I didn't want you to be hurt. That should be pretty obvious to you."

She was quiet for a moment. She sat up a bit straighter and looked at Rob intensely. "Because Matt said you have a quote 'monster crush' on me, and more," she let this second part trail off quietly under her breath.

Rob could feel blood rush to his face. He began to cough, picking up his water and taking a long drink. He set the glass down on the table between them. "Why would he say that?" he said with a nervous chuckle.

"I'm asking *you*."

Rob fidgeted in his seat. Now wasn't the time to tell Hailey...she just found out the guy she was all in on, the guy she'd even learned to cook for, had been cheating on her. And now she was more than three sheets to the wind. But isn't this how it always went? Hailey breaks up with a guy, Rob gave her space out of respect but before he can say anything, she's hooked up with a new dude. Maybe it was time to make his move.

"Hailey—"

"—are you folks ready for the check?"

The server began to clear away some of the empty dishes in front of them. Rob pressed his lips together, eyes down on his lap as he waited for the server to finish.

He cleared his throat. "Hailey—" But when he looked up, Hailey was leaning against the wall of the booth and had her eyes closed. He smiled. "Lightweight."

He got them an Uber back to her apartment and helped her walk up the steps to her unit. They were promptly greeted by one very excited Sandy. In the Uber Hailey kept talking even while half asleep.

"You're the best," she had said before resting her head against his shoulder. "What would I do without my best friend?"

Best friend. That's all you are.

He helped Hailey to her bedroom. She was mumbling something about a 5-3 double play. He had to laugh…even in her sleep and drunk she was talking baseball. A girl after his own heart. Literally. He got her to her bed. She flopped down onto the pillow. Rob took off her shoes and found a light blanket to cover her with. He brought her a glass of water and two pain relievers, helping her sit up and take them before she fell back over. He re-covered her up with the blanket and turned off her light. He sat on the side of the bed next to her. Just enough light entered the room from the rest of the apartment that he was able to see her face.

"I have more than a crush on you, always have," he said

quietly. He watched as she slept, her breath even. He wanted to curl up next to her, stay with her all night. But that wasn't a good idea.

"I lerve you," Hailey mumbled softly before rolling over onto her side, hugging a pillow to her middle.

What did she just say? I lerve you? What? Rob froze in his steps looking at the sleeping form that was his friend. *Friend.* His heart was in his throat as he left the room.

He took Sandy out for a walk. He mulled everything over in his head. He was conflicted. But one thing was for certain, it had not been the right time to talk to her while she was drunk. He was grateful the server interrupted them before he spilled the beans. But what to do next? It was the same merry-go-round. He didn't want to take advantage of Hailey being vulnerable after her relationship with Matt collapsed, but if he waited, he risked her being off to the next guy. And there was the issue of their friendship. He didn't want to ruin it. Period. "I wish I knew how she felt," he said aloud. Sandy turned around and looked at him before giving a little bark.

Best friend. That's what I am. Nothing but a best friend.

CHAPTER NINETEEN

ERASE: *A runner who is already safely on a base is "erased" by being thrown out.*

Hailey tucked her legs underneath herself and continued to read the document on her computer. She turned to Daisy. "This is very good. I only made a couple of edits; you can look them over and decide whether you want to accept the changes or not. Good job, kiddo." She lightly tugged on the girl's dark brown ponytail. Daisy gave her a bright smile in return, Sandy was snoring away next to her.

They were on Hailey's couch. Most Wednesdays Hailey picked Daisy up from school and they spent the afternoon together. Today they were working on Daisy's English paper. It had been several days since the Matt debacle. Which meant several days since she'd gotten drunk out of her mind. She thought back to the moment she'd asked him about what Matt had said. *He's got a monster crush on you.* She hadn't said the rest out loud. *He's in love with you.* Unfortunately, this is where her memory got hazy. She couldn't remember what he'd said. Had he even responded? All she *could* remember was waking up the next morning with a killer headache despite a fuzzy recollection of Rob having her take pain reliever. *Rob.* She felt a small tug in her heart at just the thought of him. And frankly, she was pretty surprised she wasn't more devastated over the Matt fiasco. She wasn't devastated at all, to be perfectly honest. It's almost as if she'd expected it. The rosy-colored glasses she'd been looking through had gotten smashed in an instant. All she could think of now were the things she hadn't liked about Matt. Didn't like dogs, didn't read, wasn't interested in the world around him other than women and baseball. What had she been thinking? It pointed her like a compass towards who she really wanted. *Rob.*

The sound of the doorbell shook her out of her daydreams.

"Hey Molls," she said as she let her friend in. Molly was in a tennis skirt and a light blue sleeveless top.

"Did you just get off work?" Hailey asked. Molly was a tennis pro at one of the posh country clubs nearby.

"Yep…I'm finished. I'll have to tell you about the hot guy who just started lessons." She waggled her brows at Hailey.

Hailey cleared her throat and nodded her head towards Daisy.

"Hey there Daisy," Molly said as she set a bag down on the table.

"Hi Miss Molly," Daisy replied, smiling broadly.

"Good Golly," Molly replied. "And you have no idea what I'm talking about." She smiled. "Frankly I'm too young to know what I'm talking about. Hailey said she was helping you with a paper. What are you writing about?" She pulled out a bottle of champagne from the bag and waved it at Hailey before putting it in the refrigerator.

"I'm writing about Frankenstein by Mary Shelley, about how the topics she explored were not usual topics for women during the Regency period," Daisy replied before returning her attention to her laptop resting on the coffee table.

Molly stopped moving for a minute. "Wow. I'm more of a Dracula girl myself, he's got that whole sexy suck your neck thing going on."

"Hey," Hailey said, looking at Molly while shaking her head no.

Daisy was giggling before suddenly looking at her cell phone. "I gotta go, my dad's downstairs. Thank you for your help Hailey," she said as she packed her things into her purple backpack. "Bye Sandy," she said, leaning down to give the small dog a kiss on his head. Sandy gazed up at her with his big brown eyes, his skinny tail swishing back and forth.

"You're welcome, sweetie. I'll see you next week." She kissed Daisy on the top of her head and gave her a big hug before watching her leave. Hailey watched until she saw Daisy climb into her dad's truck. She closed the door.

"Tell me again what that shit head did because I can't believe he did that to you." Molly stood with her hands on her hips. "Wait...let's get our pizza order in, the Lakers play tonight...Pizza Nuevo always takes forever when a game is on."

Hailey watched as Molly dug her phone out of her purse and placed their usual order of a grilled vegetable pizza with goat cheese and balsamic vinegar drizzled over the top. Once she was finished she retrieved the bottle of champagne from the refrigerator, expertly popped the cork and poured them each a glass. They curled up on Hailey's couch.

"It was awful Molls. You should have seen the bimbo he had over...*Ginger*. You know...the type to wear fishnet and thongs along with enough black eyeliner to paint a house with. Except she was in his jersey instead of the fishnet."

"Slut," Molly said before taking sip of her bubbly.

"I mean...*is* she? Maybe we should be calling Matt the

119

slut. He's the one that was supposedly in a one-on-one relationship with me but sleeping with her to break his losing streak. Seriously. He's the slut. I think we need to get away from only using that word on women, especially when it's the men that are to blame."

"Okay, okay…you know what I meant…you don't have to go all Gloria Steinem on me. I still can't believe he did it. *And* I can't believe you're taking it so well." Her eyebrows knitted down; the corners of her mouth curled down also. "I mean, why *are* you taking it so well?"

Hailey set her flute down onto her marble topped coffee table and leaned back on the turquoise colored sofa. "I'm not sure, to be honest. I keep waiting for my reaction. But there's something Matt said I didn't tell you about."

She looked over at her friend. Molly had her eyebrows lifted in surprise.

"Which is?" Molly asked.

"As I was leaving…while he was standing on his porch, still in a towel with chicken and zoodles all over his chest," she let out just the smallest giggle at the memory, "he said, and I'm paraphrasing—"

"Hailey, you're just telling *me*…I'm not the editing police…just say it."

"He said, 'go run to your friend Rob, he's got a monster crush on you.'"

Molly set her glass down next to Hailey's. She blinked a few times. "What does that mean? Do you think Rob said something to him?"

"I don't think so, because when I asked Matt, he just said it was obvious. And he said Rob was in love with me."

"What? In love? He said that?

Hailey nodded.

"But wait…why would Rob even have hooked you up

with Matt in the first place? That doesn't make any sense, although I've always suspected he liked you."

"It didn't make sense to me either until I remembered who Rob is. Rob is above all honest, proper, and above board at all times. A gentleman. He's always saying he wants to be a mensch. Which is a—"

Molly held up her hand. "I know what a mensch is. What's your point?"

"My point is that maybe Rob handed out my number because that's who he is and not necessarily what he wanted to have happen. Knowing him he probably didn't want to deny me the opportunity to date someone like Matt." She absently stroked Sandy's coat as she talked.

"Who knew he'd turn out to be a slut." Molly snorted. She got up from the couch and returned with the bottle of champaign, refilling their glasses before sitting back down next to Hailey. "So, what are you going to do about it?"

Hailey had been mulling this over all day. "I'm not sure yet."

"You've always begged off the question when I've asked you whether you had feelings for Rob, you've always brushed the question aside saying, 'we're just friends.'" Molly had a gleam in her eyes as she looked at Hailey. "Do you want it to be more than friends?"

Hailey had mulled this over maybe a thousand times since that day in the library when Rob had shown up like a knight for the princess in distress. Thinking about Matt's words filled her with bubbly joy in her heart. But a different reminder put out that joy like water on a campfire. Her dad. She'd gotten a voice mail from him that he'd been sick and wanted to see her. She hadn't laid eyes on him since she was eighteen years old and had moved out of the disaster known as their house. She'd never heard from him again. Until now. He'd rambled on in the message saying the usual cliche lines: "I know I wasn't a good father." "I don't expect you to forgive me." "I did the best I could." Being so immune to these attempted tugs at her heart-strings made Hailey feel as if she must be hardened inside to not feel something other than anger at him. She'd talked at length about this with Dr. Boone this week. She'd assured Hailey that there was no right or wrong way to feel about this. Hailey had a right to her own feelings, and they were all legitimate given her childhood. She made it clear that the decision was entirely up to Hailey as to whether she contacted her father or not. It wasn't an easy decision, and it would need to be decided on by her and her alone. Hailey truly didn't know what to do.

She let the thought go for now, picturing it in a balloon and letting it go to mull over later. One of the many helpful tools she'd learned in her several years of meditation. As soon as she let that thought balloon go another dropped down into her lap. *Rob.*

CHAPTER TWENTY

DEEP IN THE COUNT: *Whenever a third ball has been called, (3-0, 3-1, or 3-2 count), the situation favors the batter.*

"Wow." Spencer shook his head as he finished his beer. "That's kind of crazy. Poor Hailey. How's she handling it?"

Rob and Spencer had just finished a round of golf and were sitting outside of the clubhouse having lunch. It was a nice day, low eighties and not a cloud in the sky. Rob relayed the entire story of Hailey and Matt starting with Hailey's pretty good attempt at cooking and ending with Matt being covered with all of said cooking. He filled in the middle about Ginger and Matt wanting to turn his luck around. He hadn't yet told Spencer what Matt had said about him having feelings for Hailey. Which really must have been some kind of male intuition on Matt's part because Rob had never breathed a word about how he felt about Hailey to Matt. Not one single word.

"Surprisingly well, if you don't count the fact that she had several tequila shots."

"Well, it worked," Spencer said as he took a bite of his tuna sandwich, wiping his mouth with the back of his hand.

"What worked?" Rob asked taking a bite of his own turkey sandwich.

"He's hitting better. He's had three home runs the past two games. Either he does better in his own ballpark or the Dodgers should hire Ginger to help some of their other hitters. And now he's out of your way. A two for one if you ask me." He waived for the server to come to their table. "You want another?" he asked Rob, pointing to the empty beer glass in front of him.

"Sure," Rob replied. He leaned back in his chair and studied the golf course laid out in front of them. He'd had a pretty good round; he'd shot 89 which for him was one of the few times he'd broken 90. It crossed his mind more than once that maybe things were looking up for him. "There's one other thing that happened."

"What's that?" Spencer asked after nodding thanks to the server for the fresh beers.

"Matt told Hailey that she was free to be with me because I had a quote, 'monster crush' on her."

Spencer's face was pure surprise. "He said that to her?"

"Yup."

"Wow." Spencer tossed his napkin next to his plate and leaned back in the chair. "How did he know, did you talk to him or something?"

"Are you kidding? Of course not. He just seemed to know, I guess. Some kind of man-tuition."

"And Hailey told you about this? What did you say?" Spencer leaned forward and grabbed a few of the house made potato chips from his plate.

"I lucked out, after she dropped that bombshell, she kind of nodded off to sleep…. this was after about three shots of tequila." His chest clenched at the memory. He's pretty sure he would have come clean had Hailey not passed out. What other option was there? It didn't seem wise to deny it, how would he ever broach the subject again? Luckily, he had some more time to come up with a plan. They'd both avoided one another the past few days. He'd texted her Monday afternoon to see how she was doing. She'd replied that she was fine if not a bit hungover and that was it. They hadn't talked since. There was also the 'I love you' she'd mumbled hanging over him.

Spencer's mouth turned into a small smile. "What are you going to do?"

Rob let out a breath. It felt as if he'd been holding his breath underwater for an indeterminable amount of time. Having reached a definitive decision felt like oxygen to his body. Life-giving oxygen.

"I'm going to take her out to dinner and tell her everything. Kind of recreate what I had planned to do in Chicago. I'm going to tell her how I feel about her, how I've always felt about her, and that I want to be with her, that I want to be everything to her, not just her friend. And I hope I don't scare her away." He looked down at his napkin before tossing it on the table. "That's what I'm going to do."

◇

"Let me get this straight, you want Matt Harper to be assigned to someone else in the office?" Donald Schultz was one of the firm's managing partners. He was leaning back in his large leather chair in front of a gleaming chrome and glass desk. His eyes narrowed as he studied Rob. "He's your biggest signing." He leaned forward, resting his elbows on his desk.

Rob cleared the lump that was lodged in his throat. His heart was racing in his chest. He knew this was not the wisest career move he'd ever made. But it was necessary. There was no way in hell he could represent Matt. None. Not after what he'd done to Hailey. It was a matter of principle. But it was dicey for his standing in the firm.

"Correct," Rob replied. He looked down briefly before leveling his gaze back to Donald. The older man had salt and pepper hair slicked back and was in one of his absurdly expensive suits. The shelves of his office held numerous sports memorabilia. Autographed football helmets, signed baseballs in acrylic holders, photos of him and several major professional athletes over the decades. It was an intimidating space to be in.

Donald steepled his fingers together as he continued to look at Rob. "This is a highly unusual request. Care to enlighten me as to why you are asking to be relieved of someone who will undoubtably be signing one of the biggest contracts in baseball next season?"

Rob nodded his head. "It's personal, sir."

With that Donald raised his eyebrows. "Personal?"

"Yes," Rob kept his head up. He looked out the windows behind Donald. The Los Angeles skyline was perfectly clear today, you could even see out to the ocean from the large corner office.

"You are one of our best senior associates, Rob. If this were anyone else in here asking for this, I would be skinning them alive before telling them to pack up their things. But you've always been a hard worker, whip smart, and a straight shooter. So, I'm going to give this one to you. I'm not saying it won't come back to bite you at some point but I'm going to honor your request."

Rob felt relief flood through his body. "Thank you, sir. I wouldn't have asked if it hadn't been absolutely necessary.

Donald nodded his head, picking up a file indicating that the meeting was over.

CHAPTER TWENTY-ONE

S *ET THE TABLE: To get runners on base ahead of the power hitters in the lineup.*

"If he's taking you to Mina's then it can only mean one thing Hailey...he's going to profess his love for you!" Molly's face lit up like a Christmas tree. "You don't take a 'friend' to Mina's...not for dinner at least, you just don't. Oh my God, what are you going to wear? Don't wear that dress you wore for New Year's...it's way too granny...how about the strappy red one...oh wait, you wore that in Chicago... what about the pale green silk—"

"How much coffee have you had Molls? You haven't let me get in even one word yet." Hailey propped the phone up in her closet so she could see Molly's face on the screen, she had her dark brown hair pulled into a high ponytail.

"I don't know...a few cups...some energy drinks...I'm just so excited for you! You are finally, and I mean *finally* going to hook up with Rob! This is so perfect, I knew this would happen, you guys are perfect together, this is why you haven't been able to find a guy because you've been waiting for *this* guy." Molly beamed at Hailey.

"Seriously Molls, you need to dial it back a bit. First, we can't assume anything about going to Mina's…it could just be that he got a bonus or maybe he signed a new client and wants to celebrate." Hailey pulled out the pale green silk dress Molly had suggested and held it up to her body, studying her reflection in the mirror.

"Did he *say* he wanted to celebrate?" Molly's eyebrows were raised.

"Well, no."

"And, if he *did* want to celebrate, why doesn't he have someone special to celebrate it with?"

"Be—"

"Because you *are* the someone special he would want to celebrate with. Except this isn't a celebration it's a revelation or a confession or a—" Molly clasped her hands in front of her mouth, "what if it's a proposal?" She squealed an ear-piercing shriek into the phone.

Hailey dropped her chin and raised her eyes up at Molly. "Okay, now you've gone way overboard. A proposal? Get a grip Molly. Jeez. Have you been binge watching the Hallmark channel?" She resumed studying her appearance. She turned to face Molly in the screen of the phone and backed up. "Is this the dress you think I should wear?"

"Yes! Believe me, if he isn't going to propose—and I know, that's a long shot—he's going to when he sees you in this."

"I propose you throttle way back on your caffeine intake."

They chatted for a few minutes and then hung up. Hailey flopped back on her bed and stared up at the ceiling. She was thinking of all the possibilities lying before her. One possibility would be that Rob wasn't going to say anything about getting together. If he truly was attracted to her, he had effectively put a lid on it for a long time, maybe he intended to keep it there. He probably was just as worried about losing their friendship as she was. But was this what she wanted?

Did she want to spend the rest of her life secretly pining for her friend and always wondering *what if?*" Her heart and her head were both speaking now, and they were saying it was time to make a move. If Rob didn't, then she would. She was tired of waiting and wondering. She needed to know now whether Rob had the same feelings she did.

❦

They had decided to meet at the restaurant since the traffic would have been too crazy for Rob to have picked her up from her apartment. He needed to come straight from his office as it turned out, something about extra work landing on his desk. Hailey decided to take an Uber, figuring Rob could drive her home after their meal.

She got out of the car and walked to the entrance of Mina's. She was so anxious that her palms were a bit clammy, and her heart was racing. She closed her eyes and took a few deep, calming breaths before pulling the door open.

Mina's decor could be described as California elegance. The walls were paneled in wood. The back of the restaurant featured floor to ceiling windows that faced the wooded back patio. Large pots of white orchids were plentiful throughout the space. Behind the bar was a large slab of white onyx back lit in front of a shiny mahogany bar. The barstools were muted bronze metal and black leather. Hailey looked around and didn't see Rob. She fired off a quick text but when he didn't immediately respond she assumed he was driving.

She slipped onto one of the barstools and ordered a glass of chardonnay. The cheapest one was $28 but it sure did taste good. The wine washed her body in calmness as if she'd been covered with a weighted blanket. She'd decided on the green silk dress. She wore her hair in a high ponytail and accessorized with gold jewelry and high strappy nude sandals. She'd spritzed herself with a spicy vanilla Jo Malone scent layered with the orange blossom perfume. Even she was pleased with the look.

"Is this seat taken?" she heard his voice in her ear.

She spun around, coming face to face with Rob. He looked so sexy and hot in a blue blazer and white dress shirt paired with dark jeans. She put one arm around his neck and pulled him in for a hug. He smelled of wood and leather with a touch of citrus. She could have lived in his divine scent. She reluctantly pulled her face away.

"The hostess said we had a few more minutes until our table is ready," he said as he climbed onto the stool next to her and ordered an old fashion. He looked her up and down. "You look beautiful, Hailey," he said softly. His eyes were warm as he admired her. "Really beautiful." He took a swallow of his drink.

"Thank you. You look pretty good yourself," she replied through a dry throat. There was a different vibe happening between them. If she wasn't mistaken, she'd say that Rob seemed as nervous as she felt. There wasn't the normal ease between them. There was a tension going on that wasn't a bad thing.

"Mr. Steadman, your table is ready," the hostess offered to hold Hailey's glass of wine as she slipped from the bar stool. "Please follow me."

Their table was next to the window. The sun was low in the horizon and the twinkly lights of the back patio area were on. The hostess handed them menus and said their server would be with them shortly. Hailey peaked over the top of her menu to look at Rob. His eyes looked up at her at the exact same moment. They held each other's gaze for a moment before both turned their attention to the menus in front of them.

"Have you been here before?" she asked through a throat lined in cotton. She was trying not to look at the prices, but dear lord they were high.

"Once for a client lunch. I was so impressed that I tucked it away in my mind as somewhere to come back to." He looked up at her. His face softened. "Don't worry about the price of anything, Hailey, it's all my treat tonight."

"Are you sure? It's really, *really* expensive." She chewed on her bottom lip.

"I'm totally sure. My bonus at the start of the year was a big one." He smiled before looking back at his menu.

Wait. Bonus? Was this just a dinner for him to splurge at a good restaurant? He did say after having lunch here he wanted to come back...maybe that's all this was? She swallowed. She was determined. If Rob didn't say anything, then she would. She'd concluded that one of the reasons why she wasn't upset by the whole thing with Matt was because it had opened the door to the possibility of something with Rob. And that was worth more than being with anyone else. But the other reason she wasn't upset was because Matt had turned out to be a giant dud. Yes, he was a hot dud, but a dud none the less. The guy barely had two brain cells...other than baseball they had nothing in common and even baseball wasn't much of a connection because he hadn't seemed to revere the game with the same sense of history and tradition as Hailey did. He'd gotten into it for the money and to get laid. And there was the teeny tiny issue of dogs. He didn't like *them*, and Sandy didn't like *him*. Case closed.

They sat quietly as they ate their first course. Oysters in a vinaigrette with minced shallots on top. She was still sipping on the glass of wine from the bar. They talked about Rob's work. The firm seemed to be attracting a lot of new athletes lately. Rob had signed some new minor league players. She watched as he finished the last of his cocktail.

"I'm not representing him anymore," he said. He leaned back in his chair, one arm on the table.

"Who?" she asked.

"Matt. I asked that he go to someone else in the firm."

Hailey's eyes went wide. "But he was your biggest client, Rob. Why did you do that?" Her brows knit down as she twisted her napkin in her lap.

"The guy was an asshole to you, Hailey. I couldn't fairly represent him. Punch him? No problem. Represent him? Big problem."

She felt pleasure wash over her chest. Her heart felt as if it was swelling under her breastbone. But this wasn't good for his career. Hailey knew that much. "Because of me you dropped your biggest star? Rob, I don't know what to say. That makes me feel awful actually."

"Don't worry about it even for a second. It was fine."

"The partners were fine with it?" She narrowed her eyes.

"They were. He'll just go to someone else. Not really a big deal. Honestly. And even if it was, it would be okay with me."

Hailey felt a stab of anxiety pierce her entire body. The idea that Rob had jeopardized his career at his firm for her made her feel extremely uncomfortable. It was the same feeling as dreaming about showing up somewhere without clothes on. She felt exposed. She certainly wasn't deserving of this action of his.

She reached out and put her hand on his wrist. "Rob, I don't want you to sacrifice your career for me." She held his dark brown eyes with hers.

He responded by putting his hand on top of hers. "First off, it really is more about me. I couldn't in all honesty continue to represent him. What he did to you marred how I see him, I need to give my clients all of my effort and if I don't respect them as a person I just can't do that. And secondly, even if it was purely for you it would be worth it.

You're worth it." His lids were lowered, his eyes looking up at her through his lashes.

Hailey swallowed. Feelings were fighting with one another like two boxers in a ring. In one corner were her feelings of low self-worth. Despite her therapy she still struggled to feel worthy of anyone doing anything nice for her. All the negative messages her father gave her as a kid would rear their heads and kick her right in the stomach. She was constantly replaying her mantra in her head: *you are loved, you are worthy of kindness.* She slowly took a breath and looked at the opposite corner of the boxing ring where her feelings of attraction and love, yes love, for Rob stood. He was so very wonderful. She could probably live for a hundred years and never find a better man than him. When he said she was worthy of kindness and consideration it made her feel so loved and comforted in the world. His words enveloped her like a warm soft blanket, a place she never wanted to leave.

CHAPTER TWENTY-TWO

C RACK OF THE BAT: *The sound of the bat hitting the ball. The term is used in baseball to mean "immediately, without hesitation."*

Rob glanced over at Hailey in the passenger seat of his car. Dinner had been wonderful...magical. His eyes ran up and down her legs, he'd noticed those the day he'd met her. Beautiful and shapely. Every inch of her was beautiful to him. His heart had broken just a bit when she said she wasn't worth him taking a stand at work regarding Matt. He knew she'd had a tough childhood, but she didn't speak much about it. He knew she'd been abandoned by her mom at a young age, and he knew that her father had been verbally abusive and basically not available. Whenever that part of her peeked out he tried to reassure her. He wanted to make up for every terrible thing that had ever been said or done to her.

They were headed to his house, which was close to the restaurant. Rob had bought a small cottage in the Hollywood

Hills several years ago. He'd been accepted to Stanford and Harvard for undergrad and law school but had chosen UCLA for both since he'd been offered a free ride. As a result, he was student-debt free. Not only did this mean that his salary was freed up for a mortgage ,but the college money his parents had set aside for him was left untouched and he was able to use it for a down payment.

He pulled into the steep driveway and stepped out. The sky was nearly dark. It held only a few dark purple remnants from the day that had passed. He smiled at Hailey. "Would you let me open your door for you?" He noticed her cheeks flush soft pink.

"Maybe," she replied, her eyes warm and inviting.

Rob got out and sprinted around the car pulling her door open. He offered his hand as she swung her legs out. She stood up, tilting her head back to look at him. Her eyes roamed from his lips up to his eyes. He wanted to kiss her. A lot. But he should wait until they'd talked. *Right?* Was he being too cautious? Caution had kept him from ever expressing himself to Hailey. Maybe it was time to throw caution to the wind and stop being rational and logical about everything. Time to go with his heart instead of his lawyer brain.

He put a hand on the small of her back and brought his lips to hers. He saw her close her eyes and he felt her body lean into his. Her lips were soft and warm. The feeling of them against his own sent desire roaring through his entire body. He pulled back, his eyes looking into hers. He tucked a stray piece of blond hair behind her ear.

"Let's go inside," he said, taking her by the hand.

As soon as they went through the front door, they were a tangle of arms and legs. Hailey had her hands in Rob's hair, pulling his mouth down to hers. Rob had her by the waist, pulling her body into his. He buried his nose in her hair. Her vanilla orange sent engulfed him. Her hands ran under his jacket, pulling it off him. She held it up for Rob to take and he threw it over his shoulder onto the ground.

"I've been waiting so long for this, Hailey." His lips found the underside of her jaw where he sprinkled kisses all up and down her throat. His hands cupped her face as he brought his lips to hers.

She pulled back to look him in the eye. "You have?"

"Since the moment we met," he said in a husky voice.

Her face looked confused. "Why didn't you tell me?"

"Should we talk now? Or later?" He felt hungry for her, and he wanted nothing more in the world than to take her to his bedroom right then and there. But, if Hailey wanted to talk...they would talk. He'd already waited five years, what was another hour or so?

But she must have been thinking the same thing because instead of giving him an answer she stepped back towards him, her eyes on his lips and then her lips were there. On his. Her mouth was so soft and warm. She tasted like wine and chocolate. Rob couldn't get enough of her. He wanted to inhale her, envelope her, to soak her into his very being.

His hands made their way lightly up and down her arms while they kissed. He could feel goose bumps freckle her skin. When his tongue found hers, she let out a small moan that went right to his core.

"Oh my God, Hailey. You're so perfect, you feel so good in my arms. I want you so God damn much." He pulled his mouth from hers and looked into her eyes. "Do you want this too?" His heart raced as he waited for her reply.

She looked at him through half lidded eyes. Her lips were pink and swollen. She nodded slowly. "I've been wanting this for a long time too," she said. Her voice was low.

Rob took her by the hand and led her to his bedroom. He took off his shoes and began to unbutton his shirt. Hailey came right over to him, running her hands over his chest. Her head tilted back looking up at him. She stepped out of her own shoes, steadying herself by holding onto his arms. He pulled her down to the bed, she faced up to him. Leaning on his elbows, he brought his lips down to her collarbone.

"I love this area on you...it's so sexy," he murmured in between kisses. His tongue made its way lower. Hailey leaned her head back, running her hands through Rob's hair. He sat up and finished removing his shirt, throwing it onto the ground beside the bed. He could see her checking out his body. He was thankful he'd always found time to hit the gym.

He watched as she swallowed. "My God, Rob...you look so good," she said. He saw her eyes travel back to his face.

"It's all for you, baby." He gently slid down one of the thin straps of her dress.

She looked at him and slid the other one down before standing and slipping out of the dress entirely.

Rob's pulse quickened as he watched her. She was so damn sexy in a pale pink silk bra and matching panties. He watched as she took off her bra. His throat was dry just looking at her amazing breasts. Soft mounds with pale pink nipples. He'd fantasized about this moment more times than he could count but the real moment was taking his breath away. *She* was taking his breath away. He wanted to scoop her up into his arms and never let go.

He rolled onto his back, pulling her on top of him. They kissed and touched each other's bodies. His hands covered her soft skin, her sweet breath in his ear. He couldn't believe this was happening after all the years and all the time spent desiring her. She was finally about to be his.

"Are you sure you want this?" he asked. His voice was rough.

"I've never been more sure about anything," she replied. Her hands roamed over his chest and down to his belt. She undid him and slid his pants down. Her lips slowly broke into a smile.

"I take it you like what you see," Rob said, he could feel his face blush.

Hailey only nodded her head. He finished getting undressed and rolled himself on top of her, kissing his way down to her panties. He slipped his fingers under the waist of them and slowly pulled them down her thighs and off her body. He paused to admire how beautiful she looked. His mouth soon found her most heated area. Rob indulged in his desire for Hailey as he brought her to the brink of control, threading his hands through hers and pulling her right over the edge while she moaned his name.

Her body quivered and pulsed as he held her. Her nipples were hard, and a soft pink flush covered her chest. He nuzzled his mouth in her neck, sucking lightly and kissing tenderly. "I want you," she whispered in his ear.

Without a word, Rob grabbed a condom from the side table drawer and was quickly inside her. She was warm and wet and felt like home. His home. Her softness enveloped him. Before he knew it, he was experiencing pleasure as he never had before. She was perfect for him. After all the times he'd thought about having her he finally did. He brought his mouth to her ear. "God, that was amazing," he whispered. He rolled onto his side and pulled Hailey's back into his front.

"Does this make me the little spoon?" she said after a couple of quiet minutes.

He grinned. "The best little spoon ever," he replied. He pulled her hair from her cheek, sweeping it to the side of her neck. His lips found her soft skin. She smelled so damn good. He could lay here forever with her body tucked into his. Her body was small and soft.

"Do you want to talk?" she asked, pulling a light blanket over their bodies.

"Sure," he replied.

Hailey turned over and propped herself up on an elbow, facing him. She used one hand to trace something on his chest.

"Did you just write your name on me?" he asked, bemused.

She nodded her head. "I did. I'm branding you as mine." Her eyes found his.

Rob felt a surge through his body. "I'm all yours, Hailey. Always have been." He held her gaze. He knew she was being playful, but he wasn't. He was as serious as he'd ever been about anything. He was all hers. Body, soul, and mind.

"Why did you wait so long to tell me?" Her face was full of questions.

Rob cleared his throat. "I never wanted to interfere. When we first met you were heartbroken over that jerk who dumped you by text message. I figured it would have been shitty to hit on you when you were obviously vulnerable. But then before I could gather up the courage you had moved on. It seemed to be the story of my life." He leaned forward and kissed her lips.

Hailey seemed to chew on this bit of information for a bit. "I wish I would have known. I've always been attracted to you too, but I'm used to guys making it known quite bluntly if they were interested...I always figured I just wasn't your type."

Rob snorted. "You didn't think you were my type?" He brushed a piece of hair from her face. "Hailey, it's almost as if you were made for me." He drew his eyes to her lips and leaned in, lightly brushing his mouth to hers. He noticed her breath hitch. "Stay the night with me," he said, leaning back to look at her.

"I'd love to, but I can't leave Sandy alone. Plus, I don't have anything else to wear...or a toothbrush."

"I'll go get Sandy. Text me a list of what you need me to get for you." He sat up, pulling on a pair of sweats. He looked back at Hailey, lying under a blanket on his bed. Naked and beautiful. And his. Finally.

CHAPTER TWENTY-THREE

DIAL LONG DISTANCE: *To hit a home run.*

Hailey sat up on her elbows and looked around Rob's bedroom. She felt as if she were in a dream. She felt glowy and light. Things looked as if she were looking through a Vaseline smeared lens. She smiled. *Rob.* She let her head fall back onto the pillow. *Wow.* Who knew? The sex had been amazing, and the connection was so intense. It seemed like the most natural thing in the world to be in his arms… naked…in his bed.

Her core vibrated as she thought back to how his touch felt on her body. It's as if he knew her better than she knew herself. Every touch perfectly placed, every movement exactly what she wanted, every place on her body his lips had touched had been what she needed. Her body had thrummed under his fingers.

On top of being amazing in bed, he'd even gone off to collect her dog and her things. *A perfect gentleman.* She got up and pulled one of Rob's clean t-shirts from his dresser drawer. She brought it up to her nose. It smelled like Rob. Like clean laundry and cedar. She pulled the shirt over her head and shimmied back into her panties which had been tangled in the sheets that had made their way to the floor. She padded out to Rob's kitchen to get a glass of water.

His house was small but cozy and comfortable. It was one of those old Spanish bungalows that Los Angeles was known for. His kitchen was gray and white and tidy. Much more organized than her own. She took her glass of water out to the living room and sat down on his brown leather sofa. Rob's style was masculine and classic. Ralph Lauren meets the Gap. The room had a pitched beam ceiling, the fireplace was made up of small, glazed copper-color tiles, the walls painted white to contrast with the dark wood. Lamps, area rugs and throw blankets made the space inviting. Framed photos of family and friends made it homey.

Hailey pulled her phone from her purse. Molly had texted her several times.

Molly: How's it going?

Molly: Remember that if he doesn't tell you then you need to tell him. Take the bull by the horns Hailey. You've got this! (This was followed by numerous celebratory emojis.)

Molly: OMG, it's getting late...that can only mean one thing!!! Text me!!!! (Here she'd inserted fireworks and eggplant emojis.)

Hailey took a minute to decide whether she wanted to respond. It didn't feel right in some ways...she wanted to protect what just happened between her and Rob, not blast it out. She knew Molly only had her best interests at heart, but she wanted to be careful. She felt cautiously protective about what she and Rob had just shared. She wanted to keep the memory of what just happened wrapped in a special box for her eyes only. She understood Molly felt like she had a vested interest in the outcome though. Molly had been nudging her about Rob for so long. And she'd been right. *Okay, I'll throw her a bone.*

Hailey: Can't talk right now, but I just want to say that it's been really wonderful, and everything is good. Let's talk tomorrow. XXOOXX

Molly responded with another string of emojis, a red heart, the flame, and a thumbs up. Hailey had to smile to herself. She tossed her phone back into her purse and tucked her legs under herself, pulling the navy-blue throw blanket over her body. How had she not realized that Rob liked her all these years? He had always been such a gentleman that it never occurred to her that his kind and thoughtful behavior was anything more than him being the best kind of friend he could be. She hadn't realized that it was masking a five-year desire for her.

She thought about how excruciating it must have been for him when Matt asked for her phone number. She was fairly certain that ninety-nine-point nine percent of other men would have lied and told Matt she already had a boyfriend. But not Rob. He was honest to a fault. She felt her insides become warm and gooey at the thought. He had sacrificed what he'd wanted by doing what he thought was right. His desires took a backseat to the possibility that she might date a major league baseball player. He was so selfless. Her heart gave a little squeeze. She was distracted by the sound of keys in the door. Before she could even blink Sandy was racing towards her. The little sausage dog's feet were a blur.

"Sandy!" Hailey picked him up and gave him a little nuzzle before turning her eyes towards Rob. "Thank you," she said.

He gave her a wink. "Not a problem. I've got a set of stairs in the hall closet for him and a bed."

"That's so sweet," she replied, a hand to her heart.

Dachshunds were prone to back injuries given their long spines and short legs. Many injuries occurred from jumping onto and off furniture, so having a small set of stairs for

Sandy to use at Rob's was a potential lifesaver. And it was another bit of proof of just how thoughtful and good Rob was.

Rob joined her and Sandy on the couch. They sat in comfortable silence...Sandy between them. Rob stroked Hailey's hair as her back leaned against his chest. Hailey let out a yawn.

"Sleepy?" Rob asked, his breath hot on her neck.

"I am. I could sit here all night, but I need to take a shower and get myself to bed." She stood up.

"I put your bag of things on the bed," Rob said. He raked a hand through his hair. "I set out clean towels in the bathroom." His eyes smoldered as they roamed up and down her body. "I really like that shirt on you."

Hailey's cheeks flushed lightly. "I hope you don't mind that I grabbed it."

"You are welcome to anything I have," his eyes were soft.

She made her way to the bathroom, turned the water on, got undressed and stepped into the shower. The spray of the hot water on her shoulders felt divine. She stood with her eyes closed, letting her mind wander to Rob. She knew based on trips to the beach together that he had a nice body but seeing him naked had been next level. *Everything* was nice on him. Absolutely everything. The corners of her mouth curled up into a smile and heat flooded her core. *Again.*

She felt a drift of cool air and turned around to see one very naked and very excited Rob stepping into the shower with her. She let out a small whimper at the sight of him.

"I thought maybe you needed help washing your back," he said in a low voice.

She couldn't speak. His naked body took her breath away. She only nodded as she stepped back to make room for him. He leaned down and brought his lips to hers. Her arms wrapped themselves around his neck and pulled him closer.

Rob pulled back and looked into her eyes. This face that she'd looked at so many times before was familiar, yet new. He'd never looked at her before with the desire she now saw on his face.

"Oh my God, Hailey...you're so damn beautiful." He reached for the body wash, squeezing some into his hand. The cedar and peppercorn scent filled the shower. Rob began rubbing her neck, moving down to her back. Hailey let out soft moans.

"That feels so good," she mumbled. When his hands reached around to her breasts her arousal level went into overdrive. While one hand caressed a breast, the other moved lower into her folds. The movements began slow and then sped up to match her breathing. Her fingertips began to tingle, and her legs felt as if they were going to give out. Soon every nerve ending erupted at the same time, sending spasms of pleasure over her body. "Rob," was all she could say.

She turned around to face him. "What about you?"

"I'm okay...a condom may be tricky in the shower," he said, looking a bit sheepish.

"I can't leave you like that," Hailey said in a husky voice, her eyes looking down at his need for her. She ran her hand through the soap that still covered her breasts and brought that hand down to him. She gripped him softly at first. Rob's eyes closed; his breathing became more ragged as Hailey increased her tempo. It didn't take long before Rob's pleasure crashed over the edge.

"Hailey," he said bringing his eyes down to her.

He pulled her close to him, kissing the top of her head. She smiled to herself. Why hadn't they gotten together sooner? It was all she could think of.

After they finished showering and brushing their teeth Hailey slipped into one of Rob's t-shirts for bed. He came back from the kitchen in only his boxers carrying two glasses of water. He sat one down next to Hailey. He then returned with the steps for Sandy to access the bed. "I should get another set," he said as he watched the small dog make his way onto the fluffy white and navy comforter and next to Hailey.

Rob slid in next to her, pulling her back against his front. He made her feel warm and safe in his arms and she seriously never wanted to let go of this feeling. Ever.

The next morning she woke up to an empty bed. Even Sandy wasn't there. She sat up on her elbows and gazed out the window. The sun outside was bright and the sky looked clear. Fitting weather for the day after everything that happened last night. She smiled as she swung her legs from the bed. She quickly brushed her teeth and pulled her hair back into a ponytail.

She padded out to the kitchen. Rob was cooking and Sandy was on floor guard duty. Any piece of food, even the tiniest of crumbs would not escape the dog's laser focus. Rob handed her a mug of hot coffee before pulling her into him. His mouth nuzzled her neck. "Good morning," he whispered into her ear before pulling away and looking at her. His eyes sparkled in a way she'd never seen them do before. "Blueberry pancakes and bacon, okay?" he asked as he returned to the stove.

"Perfect," Hailey replied, sitting at one of the barstools at the counter. She watched his backside as he continued to cook. The butterflies in her stomach got busy again when she thought back to last night and his naked body next to hers, his naked body in the shower...soaping her up. She closed her eyes and smiled.

Rob set a plate of pancakes topped with maple syrup and a small plate of bacon in front of her before sliding onto the stool right next to the one she was sitting on. The brush of his thigh against hers caused her heart to flutter behind her breastbone. He had an additional piece of bacon cooling on a napkin. One look at Sandy sitting back in his beg-mode and Hailey knew who the piece was for.

"Thank you," she said before taking a bite. "Oh my God, these are so good." She chewed happily. "I could get used to this," she said, taking a bite of her bacon.

"I hope you do," he rasped. He leaned over and kissed her. His lips tasted like syrup and coffee.

They decided to spend the day hiking in Griffith Park. Sandy's small legs limited them to the easy trails. When they were finished they found one of their favorite taco trucks and ate at one of the many picnic tables sprinkled around it. Sandy was kept well fed and had plenty of water, falling asleep in the shade of the table.

Rob wiped his hands on a napkin before reaching across the table and taking one of Hailey's hands in his. He was in a gray surf shop t-shirt and had a Dodger's cap on his head. "This has been the best twenty-four hours of my life," he said to her. His brown eyes looked at her. She noticed for the first time the very tiny flecks of gold in them. "I wish from the bottom of my heart that I would have had the nerve to say something sooner. If I had we might be..." he trailed off. "Never mind. I'm just happy that you feel the same." He chuckled. "Of course, you know this means we can't be friends anymore." He waggled his eyebrows at her.

"Why would you say that?" Hailey set the remaining taco down in front of her. Her eyes were wide.

"I'm just kidding. Of course we're still friends. Isn't that the best part? We get to be together *and* still be friends?"

Hailey nodded. But something burrowed its way into her gut. In the glow over everything last night she'd not really considered yet whether being in a relationship with Rob would change their friendship. *It had to. Right?*

CHAPTER TWENTY-FOUR

LEAR THE BASES: A batter who drives home all the runners on base without scoring himself is said to "clear the bases."

The past two weeks had been perfect. Beyond perfect really. Rob smiled to himself as he packed up his files for the night. He and Hailey had spent every single night together. They'd settled into something that was anything but routine. It was a daily existence that Rob thrived on and loved. And speaking of love...he hadn't said those words yet to her.

They'd exchanged those words while in their 'friends-only' era, but it wasn't the same as this. It was a completely different zip-code to tell her he was *in love* with her, hell it was a completely different country. He wasn't sure what he was waiting for. He'd known it for a long time, day one really. He didn't want to scare her off because although things were out in the open and they had confessed their feelings to one another, it felt to him as if Hailey was holding back just a bit. It was as if these feelings were new to her and she was still testing them on for size, or maybe she wasn't

100% sold on them. For this reason, Rob proceeded a bit cautiously.

For the first time since they'd gotten together two weeks ago, they were going to spend the evening with his family. His mom had invited them both to dinner along with David and Hannah, and his grandparents. Rob was looking forward to it. His mom had been overjoyed when he'd shared the news with her. Hailey had been around his family before, for dinner and different celebrations, but this would be different. She'd be there now as his girlfriend.

Hailey had been the one to ask if they were going to be exclusive. The question took him by surprise because from his vantage point it seemed assumed. But again, this was based on *his* way of viewing the situation. It seemed as if Hailey still needed reassurance when Rob already had the next few years mapped out in his head. Actually, he had the rest of his life with her figured out. Yes, two weeks of being together was not long at all, but he'd been by her side for five years waiting for this moment in time. He already knew how he felt about her. The question was whether she felt the same. Could she see the rest of her life with him?

He got to Hailey's apartment. When she opened the door happiness soaked him from head to toe, like a winning coach drenched in Gatorade.

"Hi," he said, leaning in to lightly kiss her on the lips.

"Hi," she replied, her eyes dancing.

He felt small feet on his leg and looked down at Sandy, who was looking up at him, wagging his tail.

"It's as if he knows where he's going," Rob laughed.

"He knows because I told him to get ready for some Grandma Ruth spoiling."

At the mention of the name Sandy let out an ear-piercing bark and spun in a circle. Rob and Hailey laughed while Rob grabbed the dog's leash. Hailey grabbed a bottle of wine in a gift bag and her purse before they got into Rob's car and headed to his childhood home.

"I'm nervous," Hailey said quietly.

Rob looked over at her and put a hand on her knee. "You've met everyone before, nothing to be nervous about," he replied. He saw her chewing on her bottom lip.

"I know, but this is different. Maybe everyone will look at me through a different lens now that we're together. It makes sense that they would look at me differently." She absently stroked one of Sandy's ears.

"Hailey, my family adores you. They were ecstatic when I told them. The entire reason for this dinner is to welcome you into the family." The red light changed to green, and Rob turned his eyes to the road.

"Into the family? What do you mean?" Some of the color drained from her face.

"You know what I mean...as my girlfriend. I haven't brought a girl home to meet my parents since high school."

Hailey looked at him wide-eyed. "Since high school? Why not?"

"That was my last serious relationship. We broke up shortly after we both went to college." The car came to another stop.

"Why haven't you brought anyone home since?" She was still chewing on her lip and Rob wanted to sooth all her worries.

"Never met anyone I wanted to bring home. Other than you." He pulled the car up in front of his parents' house. "It's always been you, Hailey." He looked down at her mouth. He rubbed her cheek with his thumb. "From the minute I met you, it's only been you that I've wanted to bring here." He leaned in, softly brushing his lips against hers. "Don't be nervous. They already love you like family."

As soon as they got through the front door Rob's mom

had Hailey wrapped in a warm embrace. Lois leaned back and smiled at her. "I'm so happy for you, my dear." She smiled warmly.

Two seconds later Rob's grandma Ruth floated into the room, she too pulled Hailey in for a big hug. "Hello dear, we're so happy you and Robbie are together." She beamed at Hailey as she held each of her hands. Eventually she looked down at Sandy who was trying his best to be patient for his time with Grandma Ruth. "And I've got just the thing for you my little boychik. I made some noodle kugel just for you." Rob watched as Sandy followed close on his grandmother's heels for his special treat.

They traveled to the den and said hello to Rob's father and grandfather along with David and his wife Hanna. Rob's mom and grandma each hooked elbows with Hailey and guided her back to the kitchen with them. Rob was shooed out. He sat in the living room with the rest of the family and Sandy. They made small talk, but Rob's thoughts were on Hailey. It made him immensely happy to see his family take her into the fold. He knew Hailey didn't have any family except for her dad whom she didn't see or talk to as far as he could see. He hoped Hailey liked the idea of his family taking her in.

Dinner was good, as usual. His mom and grandma were excellent cooks. Rob knew Hailey had been in there with them, maybe they were passing on cooking tips. Just the thought warmed him. Hannah hadn't ever taken to any of the impromptu cooking lessons and eventually his mom and grandma gave up. Hannah was busy with work, and her and David usually ate out or got food delivered. He'd heard his mom and grandma tsk about this on more than a few occasions. Jewish moms and grandmothers were all about feeding their families...Rob knew the thought of David existing on take-out gave his mom fits. Some people might see this as a parent being too overbearing, but Rob wouldn't trade it for anything in the world. It was family looking out for one another and family making sure you knew you were never alone. Ever.

CHAPTER TWENTY-FIVE

INSURANCE RUN: *A run scored by a team already in the lead.*

"I have to leave early in the morning, I have an early phone call with a new client. I'll try not to wake you. Unless you want me to stay at my place tonight." Rob looked at her.

They were at a stoplight, having just left his family's house.

"That's fine. You know me, I don't wake easily. Is this your new client...the one from Japan?" She nodded her head forward as the light had just turned green.

"It is. We have a conference call at 6am, which is 7pm for him."

They were both quiet for a minute.

"Did you have a good time tonight?" Rob asked.

It had been a great evening. She had been surprised by just how differently his family had treated her. Especially Rob's mom and grandmother. They had always been warm and friendly to her, but this had been different. They'd pulled her into the kitchen with them. Evidently Rob had shared with them her recent foray into cooking. His mom presented her with an apron with her name embroidered on the top. She said it would be Hailey's to use at their house whenever she was over. It had been such a sweet gesture. The permanence of it embedded itself into Hailey's heart. It was if his mom was saying that she belonged there and that she had a home there.

His grandmother and mom had given her some simple cooking tasks and did their best to share cooking tips. It seemed silly really, but it had made Hailey feel like a daughter. Something she hadn't felt in quite a long time, if ever, really. She felt the hot tear travel down her face. And then she felt Rob's hand wipe it away.

"Hey, are you okay?" Although they were still several blocks from his apartment, he pulled over to the curb, stopping the car. He turned towards her. "What's wrong?"

She looked at his face. His warm brown eyes were looking at her. His hair was slightly messy and his normally clean-shaven face was now showing hints of stubble. She could feel more hot tears ready to spill down her cheeks.

"I'm just not used to having anything that feels like family," she said. She looked down at her lap. Sandy was looking up at her with eyes full of concern.

Rob took both of her hands in his. "Look at me Hailey."

She looked up into his warm eyes. Coffee colored pools she'd looked at countless times before. But this was different.

"You have a family now," he said in a quiet voice. "My family adores and loves you, Hailey." His hand smoothed over her hair and drew her face into his chest. She sobbed as he rubbed her back. "*I* adore and love you."

Hailey tipped her head back and looked into his eyes.

"I love you, Hailey. I've loved you from the second I met you. I'm in love with you and will be for the rest of my life." He steadied his gaze at her.

"Oh Rob," she said, wrapping her arms around his neck. "Thank you."

"Don't thank me, it's true."

She pulled away and drew her own eyes towards his. "I love you too." She leaned towards him, kissing him fully and passionately.

He drew back and raised his eyebrows at her. "Let's hurry up and get back to your place," he said, pulling the car back out onto the street.

Hailey smiled. She ran her hand down the back of his neck, stopping to touch a piece of his hair. "Sounds good," she said.

When she awoke the next morning Rob was gone. He'd left a note on his pillow.

I love you.

She smiled and swung out of bed. "Let's go for our walk Sandy."

Forty minutes later she was back at her apartment, a coffee cup in hand. She poured some kibble into Sandy's dog dish and pulled a box of cereal from the cupboard. She had her phone in one hand and fired off a text to Rob.

Hailey: Love you too.

She watched the three dots moving along the screen.

Rob: Lucky me.

Hailey spent the remainder of the morning working on her latest job. It was a murder mystery and was quite good, it just needed some good copy editing. It was early afternoon before she got up and stretched. Sandy was in a spot of sun, curled up. She needed to take him for a bathroom break soon. She grabbed her phone and saw that she'd missed a call from an unfamiliar but local number. The person had left a voice mail message.

Hailey...this is your dad.

Her stomach dropped. She instantly was transported

back to being a small girl as soon as she heard that voice. Her insides felt liquidy and her stomach felt like it would give way.

I haven't heard from you since I sent the email. I thought I would call. Maybe you didn't get the email. I don't know. Maybe you want nothing to do with me. That's fine too.

His voice was weak, yet gruff.

And that was it. There wasn't any 'love you' or 'I'm sorry I was such a shitty parent.' Nothing like that. She sank into a chair and ran over the message in her mind. She thought about how very different Rob's family was from hers. For one thing he had lots of family. Mom, Dad, brother, sister-in-law, grandparents. Hailey only had her dad, and he was a dad in name only. The other difference was how very much Rob's family loved and supported him. And now they loved and supported her. In a way it was like winning the family lottery. Instant family.

Her thoughts began to get dark. Her father's intrusion into her life brought dark storm clouds with it. What if ultimately Rob's family became disappointed in her too? What if they saw through to who she *really* was...a girl who's own mother hadn't wanted her. A girl whose father didn't love her. An unlovable girl. At that moment it didn't feel like an *if* but a *when*. She knew all the positive messages she'd learned in therapy, and some of it, maybe even most of it she'd adopted. But there was one thing that she'd never been able to square up. The fact that she'd come from bad parents. Didn't that make her inherently bad too? It had to.

That night she'd put on a happy face with Rob, listening to him talk about his day and his new client...a Japanese phenom and for a while she'd forgotten about her concerns. But then Rob told her about a phone call from his mom that day. He relayed to her how much his mom gushed about

Hailey and how happy they were now that they were a couple. Hailey smiled, but her mind wandered.

That night she lay next to Rob. She could hear the rhythmic quality of his breath. She loved him. A lot. But she was at the beginning of a destructive downward spiral. She was certain hearing her father's voice had triggered it. The messages of self-doubt washed over her like a rogue wave. It didn't matter that she'd spent years in therapy, just the sound of that man's voice had stripped her of every single layer of protective covering she'd applied to herself over the years. The strips and strips of self-worth she'd carefully applied like decoupage over the wounds. But the wounds were still there. They burned so hot they ignited all the protections, disintegrating them.

She finally drifted off into a fitful sleep, and when she awoke, she knew what she needed to do.

CHAPTER TWENTY-SIX

R AINOUT: *A rainout refers to a game that is canceled or stopped in progress due to rain.*

Rob ran a hand down his face and re-read the message, it had been short and sweet...

Hailey: I need some time.

That was it, the entire message. It felt like a gut punch. *What is going on?*

He tried to call but it went straight to voice mail. When he tried to text back, he got the notice that she'd silenced notifications. *What the hell happened?*

He paced around his office, eventually sitting down, his mind going in a thousand different directions at once. He swiveled his chair and looked out through his small office window. Smog and buildings. But he wasn't looking. He was going over every single thing he'd said over the past few weeks. Every single thing he'd said last night. He sifted through mountains of words, moments, and actions. It had all been good. *Really good.* At least he'd thought it had been. What on earth could be the matter?

He turned back to his desk and sat still for a few moments. Okay...maybe the newness of what they were doing caught up with her? Maybe she needed some time to process it all. They had been friends for so long and although Rob's feelings for Hailey had been crystal clear from day one, perhaps hers for him hadn't. Maybe the transition from the friends to lovers category was giving her pause.

He tapped his fingertips on his desk. But...she'd told him she loved him. *Loved* him loved him. His heart began to feel a tug, as if it were being pulled into his stomach or maybe it was being ripped straight out of his ribcage. Maybe this is what she did. Didn't she normally move through boyfriends the same way that Sandy plowed through his kibble? He'd always thought that the relationships hadn't gone very far. A few dates max. These past few weeks had been a great deal more than just a few casual dates. He shook his head and furrowed his brows. Did he really know the extent of her previous relationships? He thought he did. But maybe he didn't.

The thought that he'd just gotten her and now could lose her crashed over Rob like an avalanche. He couldn't breathe. *No. God no, please.* He picked up his cell phone and tried her number again. Straight to voice mail.

"Hailey, I'm not sure what's happened or why exactly you need space away from me. I just need you to talk to me. Please." He paused for a few seconds. "I love you, Hailey. Please talk to me." He disconnected. If she needed time, he could do that. It was going to be damn difficult, but he could do it. He needed to busy himself with work and let time go by. Have trust in his gut that she really did love him and that this was nothing more than what her words had said...she needed time. He hoped like hell she'd come back to him. He needed her.

CHAPTER TWENTY-SEVEN

C ROSSED UP: *When a catcher calls for the pitcher to throw one type of pitch, but the pitcher throws another, the catcher has been crossed up.*

"Hailey, it's me, open the door. I know you're in there."

Hailey didn't move from the couch. She could hear Molly's voice but couldn't move. Her mood had circled down the drain the past two days. Instead of being able to pick herself back up as she'd done in the past all she could hear were the negative messages. The bad ones. Her psyche was picking out every little scrap of evidence she'd ever come across that said she wasn't lovable. Most recently: Matt. Look what happened there. She hadn't been worth his devotion despite what he told her.

"Hailey...I'm going to use my key to come in...because I'm worried about you."

Hailey could hear the lock click and the door open. Sandy only briefly looked up from his station on the couch. He'd been her faithful little sentry during the past two days; he'd kept watch over her. Dogs loved you no matter who you were. That thought squeezed her heart.

"Oh sweetie...what's going on?" Molly sat on the ground next to Hailey. "Rob called me. He's worried sick about you."

Hailey started to speak but the tears trickled down before she could get even one word out.

"What happened? Did Rob do something? Because you know I'll murder him if he did." Molly brushed some hair from Hailey's forehead.

Hailey shook her head no. She couldn't speak. Not without the waterworks taking over.

"Okay...well...let's at least get you cleaned up. Taking a shower will make you feel worlds better. I promise."

Molly helped her up off the couch and pulled her to the bathroom. She turned on the hot water and rummaged around for a clean towel. "I'm going to take Sandy out for a walk. I brought you pho from that place down the street you love. It's on the counter. I'll be back in about 30 minutes. Sandy looks like he could use the fresh air." Molly looked at her, running a hand over her shoulder as Hailey got undressed. "I brought you some new body wash...I thought you might like the scent...and the bottle's pretty. Will you be okay while I'm gone?" Her eyes were soft.

Hailey nodded yes before stepping into the hot shower. She heard Molly talking to Sandy and then heard the front door close. She stood with her forehead against the tiled wall of the shower. The hot spray was covering her back. She turned her head and eyed the bottle of a fancy citrus smelling body wash. She wasn't even sure she deserved a friend like Molly.

She'd had episodes of depression like this in the past, but it had been quite some time since the last one. She'd stupidly thought that maybe they wouldn't occur any longer since she'd come so far in her therapy and practiced meditation faithfully. But she hadn't been spared from the clutches of depression once more. She knew she should be calling Dr. Boone, but she just hadn't even been able to muster up the energy. And Rob. He'd left several messages, but she hadn't listened to any of them.

She used the body wash to clean herself. The grapefruit scent filled the bathroom. Next, she washed and conditioned her hair. She even shaved her legs. She turned the water off and wrapped herself in the clean towel Molly had left next to the shower. She did feel a bit better. She was certain she smelled better. But she still felt that pit in her stomach. That lead anchor that was keeping her tethered down.

She pulled on some soft sweatpants and a clean t-shirt and padded out to the kitchen. Molly *had* gotten her favorite pho and it smelled heavenly. She pulled down a soup bowl and prepared the dish. The delicate and aromatic broth warmed not only her body but also her mood. She added a squeeze of lime, a handful of the Thai basil leaves, and added some hot sauce to the soup and stirred it around. She was a few bites in when Molly and Sandy returned. Sandy came running up to Hailey, putting his small paws on her leg. His big brown eyes looked up at her as if to see whether the shower and soup had helped. His small face filled with unconditional love squeezed at her heart.

"So glad you showered," Molly said, pouring herself a glass of sparkling water. "You were kinda stinky." She wrinkled her nose while pouring a second glass of water, giving it to Hailey.

"Thank you," Hailey said softly, before taking another bite of the soup. "Thank you for everything."

Molly sat down across from her. "Of course. What are friends for?" She put one hand up as a stop sign. "I know, I know, they're for borrowing clothes, taking your make-up, calling you to come pick them up at one in the morning when you're too drunk to drive." She grinned. "Honestly, I'm glad you're back among the living." Molly nibbled on a spring roll. "What happened?" Her eyes looked across the table at Hailey.

"Nothing *happened*." Hailey looked down into her bowl. "I just got scared. I *am* scared."

"Of what?" Molly prodded gently.

For all the times Molly could be blunt and balls-to-the walls, she could also be like this. Kind, soft, and thoughtful. It's the part that has kept them friends over all these years.

"I don't want to disappoint him." Hailey swirled the broth with her spoon.

"That would be impossible," Molly replied. "Rob adores you."

Hailey swallowed and set her spoon down on her napkin. "But I *will* disappoint him. Eventually." She took a deep breath and slowly let it out through pursed lips. "My mother abandoned me; my father couldn't stand me…how could I not be inherently bad?"

Molly looked at her with kind, soft eyes. "But you're not inherently bad. You're not bad at all. You know this, Hailey. You had piece of shit parents, that doesn't make you a piece of shit." She came and sat next to Hailey, putting her hand on her arm. "You are not your parents." Molly stood up and moved behind Hailey. She gathered her still damp hair in her hands, and slowly began to braid it. "It's that whole nature vs. nurture stuff. And this is what I believe on the subject, for what it's worth. I believe we all come into this world as a fully formed person as far as personality, traits, and talents are concerned. It's parents and your environment that then help these to blossom or wither. You *are* who you are because that's how you were born, you came into this world as a kind, sweet, smart woman, and it's *despite* your parents that you're as good as you are Hailey." Molly kissed the top of Hailey's head.

"That's kind of what Dr. Boone says also," Hailey said, sniffling.

"See...there you go. And Rob loves *you* Hailey."

Hailey nodded her head a bit. "I don't know Molly. I'm just so afraid to fuck up his life. He comes from such good stuff. And I don't. I'm afraid to be a parent and I know Rob wants kids...he'll be a great father. But me? How do I know if I'll be a good parent? Maybe that's when all the lack of nurture will rear its head...if I become a mom." She dried her eyes with a tissue, crumpling it up into her hand.

"Look how you are with Daisy," Molly said. She took a sip of water.

"That's more like a big sister really," Hailey replied.

"But the point is that you are great at it and...it's the same stuff...love and support. I've seen you with Daisy countless times and you're always terrific. I know for a fact that Daisy's life is better because she has you. Not to mention what a great dog mom you are to Sandy. You take better care of him than you do yourself most days."

Hailey took a sip of her own water, setting it back down as she ran things around in her mind. "I just don't want to wind up ruining his life, Molls. He's too good to have that happen to." She looked down at her lap. "He's much too good."

Molly came around to her and took one of Hailey's hands in hers. "You're much too good to deny yourself this." She kissed Hailey's forehead. "I've got to go. Will you be okay?"

Hailey nodded her head. "Thank you, Molls."

Molly gathered her purse and looked at Hailey. "Of course. Please call me if you need anything."

Once the door had closed Hailey took the glass of water and returned to the couch, curling her legs up underneath her and covering herself with the soft white throw she kept on it. Sandy made himself at home next to her. He gave her hip a nudge with his nose. She looked down at his deep brown eyes. "Am I a good mommy to you, Sandy?" The dog didn't know what she was saying but he wagged his thin tail just the same. Hailey let out a shuddered breath before leaning down and kissing the small dog on his head. "Let's watch some baseball...just not the Dodgers." She didn't need to see Matt and be reminded of her shortcomings. She was well aware of those.

CHAPTER TWENTY-EIGHT

IMMACULATE INNING: A half-inning in which the pitcher strikes out all three batters he faces with exactly nine pitches.

Rob flopped down on his couch and began to mindlessly flip through the television channels. Maybe a good baseball game would take his mind off Hailey and from his brain's endless speculation as to why exactly she wasn't speaking to him. The clicker stopped on the Dodger game. They were playing the Diamondbacks. He kept clicking through...he certainly didn't need to see that asshole Matt.

Fuck. He finally got Hailey and then promptly lost her. He kept going over in his brain what exactly could have gone wrong. He couldn't find a damn thing. Nothing. He could only guess that it was something wholly unrelated to him. Something within Hailey...something she was struggling with. He knew she struggled with her moods sometimes. It usually seemed to be related to something from her childhood or her constant relationship jumping which always left her feeling blue and empty. But Rob was usually pulled into the folds of these moods. He *had* been the one she'd turn to in order to feel better…to be comforted by him. But now she wasn't talking to him and it was destroying him.

Shit. Maybe being in a relationship had fucked things up. What was happening was exactly what Hailey had been worried about. No relationship and no friendship. He hadn't ever felt this undone. He ran a hand through his hair and closed his eyes. He felt the vibration of his phone in his pocket. His eyes flew open and registered the caller's ID.

"Molly, hi," he said, sitting up ramrod straight. "Is Hailey, okay?" Adrenalin coursed through his body.

"She's okay, Rob. I wanted to talk to you though…because I think she needs you," Molly sighed.

"What's going on?" Rob stood up and began to pace.

"I'm not sure if Hailey shared with you that her dad has been in contact with her lately."

Rob could feel his jaw tighten immediately. *What did this asshole do now?* "No. She hadn't said anything to me." Rob walked around his living room.

Molly was quiet for a second. "A few weeks ago he'd reached out to her via email. He said he was sick, and he thought maybe she would see him."

"Unbelievable," Rob growled. "He basically let her raise herself, tore down her self-esteem and yet now that he's sick he wants to see her? I hope she told him to go fuck himself." Rob's chest felt as if it was going to explode.

"She didn't. But she didn't respond either. She just ignored the email. But then he left a voice mail last week and now—" her voice trailed off.

"Now what? What has that piece of garbage done now?" Rob's free hand clenched into a fist. He was usually a chill kind of guy but the thought of this poor excuse of a father trying to get back into Hailey's life and upsetting her made him want to commit acts of violence on the man.

"He's dying." Molly went on to explain how Hailey had gotten a call from a hospice worker. The woman told her that her father was in his 'last moments' and that he'd asked to see her.

It felt like a boulder was crushing his chest. "How's she taking it?" he asked, eyes closed imagining what Hailey was going through. He rubbed the bridge of his nose with one hand.

"I don't know. She left to go over there about thirty minutes ago. I thought she could use your support."

Rob's eyes flew open, stunned. He couldn't believe Hailey had actually gone to see her father.

"She refused to let me go with her," Molly said, letting out a big sigh.

"I'm already out the door," he said to Molly. "Thanks." He grabbed his keys and punched the address Molly had just texted to him into maps on his phone. He needed to get to her. She couldn't face this alone.

He found the hospice facility and luckily was able to quickly secure a parking spot. He raced into the lobby, making a beeline for the check-in desk. Out of the corner of his eyes he caught a glimpse of blond hair under a Dodgers cap. He stopped in an instant. *Hailey.*

In a second he was by her side, arms around her, pulling her tight against his body. "I'm here for you," he said quietly.

Hailey's small shoulders shook. She leaned back and looked at him. Her eyes were red and swollen. Her cheeks flushed and wet with tears. "He's gone," she said in a whisper. "And because I became paralyzed over whether I wanted to see him or not he died alone." She buried her face in his neck. His nose inhaled the vanilla and orange scent of her he'd been missing this past week.

"It's not your fault, Hailey. Frankly I'm surprised you even came down here after everything he's put you through." He pulled her cap off from her head and smoothed her hair.

"I really didn't know what to do, Rob," she said. "He'd been reaching out to me, and I'd been ignoring him. And now—" she didn't finish her sentence. "He shouldn't have been alone," she let out a shaky breath. "I feel like my final act as a daughter was to let him down." She looked down at her hands which were folded neatly in her lap.

Rob leaned his head down, his eyes finding hers. "Listen to me Hailey. You have nothing, and I mean nothing, to feel bad about. That man in there—" he sat up a bit, trying to compose himself. "That man in there didn't even do the bare minimum for you as a child. He didn't do the bare minimum for you as an adult either. As far as I'm aware of, he's never once apologized, he's never once tried to make amends, he's never once tried to be a decent human being to you even. He, frankly, had a lot of nerve asking you to be there at the end for him." He took her chin in one hand and tilted her face up to his. "So don't you ever, *ever* feel bad about this." He pulled her into a tight hug. He wanted to make her better. He wanted to erase the pain and make her whole again. "I love you. You have a family who loves and adores you. *My family. Me.*"

Hailey met his eyes with hers. He ran a thumb over her cheeks, wiping away the tears that were trickling down.

"Let me love you Hailey. Please."

She nodded her head and threw her arms around his neck. He brought his mouth to her ear. "God, I've missed you. I love you, always and forever." He pulled her tight against him. He never wanted to let go of this woman. He wanted to hold on for the rest of his life.

CHAPTER TWENTY-NINE

TRIPLE CROWN: *A batter who (at the season's end) leads the league in three major categories: home runs, runs batted in, and batting average.*

"Oh my God this is so good!" Hailey's eyes closed as she swallowed. Rob's mom and grandma Ruth had made her a big container of matzo ball soup. Hailey had been practicing a few days of self-care since the day her father died. Slowly she was beginning to feel like herself. Rob had taken some time off from work and was staying with her. He'd made sure she had food, kept her apartment clean, walked Sandy, and had driven her to see Dr. Boone.

"Remember that time I made matzo ball soup for you?" Rob asked, pushing the bridge of his glasses back. He took a bite of one of the matzo balls floating in the bowl.

Hailey snorted. "Those matzos were so dense they had sunk to the bottom like cannon balls." She glanced up at Rob's wounded face. Her face softened as she reached for his hand. "But it was the sweetest gesture." She ran a hand down one of his cheeks where several days' worth of stubble had taken over.

"Yeah…you had been sick as a dog and my parents and grandparents were gone on a cruise. Mom had sent me some vague instructions to follow…since it was the kind of recipe that wasn't written down. Her and Grandma just make it from memory."

Hailey nodded. "Impressive, really."

"You'll be able to cook like that one day. They'll make sure of it." Rob smiled softly at her.

They continued to eat in silence.

"I need to swing by my place and pick up some fresh contact lenses and a few other things. Do you need me to get you anything?" Rob stacked up their bowls and took them to the sink in Hailey's kitchen.

"Boo…I like you in your glasses. You are rocking a super sexy Clark Kent look in them."

"Does that make you Lois Lane?" He arched an eyebrow.

"Yep, and you're my Superman."

Rob let out a laugh. "Did you see that new article in The Athletic? They ranked the best pitchers of all time."

Hailey came into the kitchen and crossed her arms across her chest. "I'm guessing by the fact that you're bringing this up that Randy Johnson is, in their misguided impression, listed as number one."

Rob looked over his shoulder from the sink while he rinsed dishes. "Misguided? These are professionals Hailey; these rankings are done with the same attention to detail and controlled methods as scientific research is done. You aren't going to argue with science, are you?"

"I'm going to argue with the knuckleheads at the Athletic, that's who I'm going to argue with. How can any rationally minded person think Randy Johnson is better than Sandy Koufax? How?"

Rob chuckled. "Just saying. I'm not the only one who thinks so."

She walked over to him standing at the sink and wrapped her arms around his waist, resting her cheek against his back. He felt good. Really good. The past few days had been rough, but Rob had been by her side every minute. Making sure she showered, ate, practiced her meditation, and forced her at least once a day to walk with him and Sandy, even if just for a few minutes. He kept telling her that she needed sunshine and fresh air.

At night they cuddled on the couch together, a cozy threesome with Sandy somewhere in the mix. They binged on Netflix and ate ice cream and popcorn. At night Rob held her close to his body. She felt safe lying in his arms. He made her feel loved and lovable. He respected her need to process her feelings, even if that had meant that for the first two nights, they'd never gotten beyond first base. But last night was different. She needed him. She'd reached over and touched him as he slept, overwhelmed with a need to feel him inside of her. It had been perfect, the crying that had come with their lovemaking had been cathartic. She woke up feeling a thousand times better. For the first time she could actually see her way through this dark cloud that she'd been living inside of. The dark cloud that wouldn't allow her to see two inches in front of her. The dark cloud that had made everything around her disappear, forcing her to sink within herself. But it was breaking up and she could see the bright blue sky coming through. She couldn't be happier.

CHAPTER THIRTY

WENT DEEP: *Hit a home run.*

"What time is everyone coming?" Rob called out from the backyard.

Summer was in full swing and they were having a small get together at Rob's house. Nothing too elaborate, a taco and tequila station was set up in one corner. Rob had strung twinkly lights over the overhang and Hailey had spent the past few days getting planters full of flowers and cleaning the patio furniture. She'd added an outdoor rug and some new pillows.

She flopped down on the turquoise cushioned sectional and looked at her watch. "In about 30 minutes." As she stared at Rob, she felt warmth travel across her chest and down her core. She loved him so much. It had been a tiny bit surprising how easily they'd fallen into a comfortable routine. After years of being friends the transition into lovers had been an easy one. She'd finally come out of her dark place and things had been good. Rob's family had been so supportive and loving.

"Spencer knows that Molly will be here tonight, right?" She called out to Rob as he fiddled with an outdoor speaker.

"Yep. He said he would quote 'put on his big boy clothes,'" Rob laughed. He gave the speaker a final nudge before seeming satisfied. He brushed his hands together and walked over to where Hailey was sitting. His eyes caught hers. "Have a told you how beautiful you look?" The corners of his mouth curled up slightly.

"I don't think so," she said. She smoothed out the front of her white cotton sundress with tiny yellow polka dots. She wore red strappy wedge sandals and gold hoops on her ears.

Rob sat next to her and put his arms around her shoulders. He began kissing her neck. "God, you smell so good," he said, his mouth moving to her lips. "How long did you say we have?" His hand was making its way up the inside of her thigh.

Hailey closed her eyes and made a small moan. "We don't have time," she said, her eyes opening and looking into his dark brown ones.

"Sure we do," he said, pulling her by the hand to his bedroom.

"But you're going to mess me up," she protested, smiling at him as he pulled her along.

"I don't care," he growled. "I'll give you a nice glow, I promise." He began to slide the straps of her dress down once they were in the bedroom.

But before he could go any further, Sandy began making a huge fuss in the other room, the kind of fuss he only made when someone was at the door.

Rob's chin fell to his chest. He looked up at Hailey and let out a deep sigh. "We're wrapping this party up quickly tonight." He leaned in and kissed her on the lips. His breath was minty. He raised his eyebrows at her. "Because I can't wait to have you,' he said, his voice low.

"Agreed," Hailey said, her eyes dancing.

But the party didn't wrap up quickly. They had fun with their friends until late in the evening. Rob's parents made a brief appearance, his grandparents declined saying this sounded like a party for the youngsters. David and Hannah were there. It was a really fun evening. Even Molly and Spencer had called a truce. Hailey saw them talking together for at least an hour...each seemed to be enjoying the company of the other. She'd elbowed Rob and he'd followed her eyes to them sitting in a quiet corner, laughing. Hailey and Rob had looked at each other.

"Cat's and dogs, getting along," Rob had said. "What's the world coming to?"

❦

Rob closed the front door. "Finally, I have you to myself." He looked at Hailey and waggled his eyebrows. "I hope you're not tired," he said before taking a seat next to her on the couch.

She opened her eyes and looked at him. "Too tired to clean up, but not for other things," she replied with a sly smile of her own. The evening had been a lot of fun and Hailey was filled with happiness and joy.

"Be right back," Rob said.

She watched as he left the room. She stroked Sandy's head and closed her eyes. A minute later she heard Rob walk back into the room. She opened one eye and looked at him. His arms were behind his back. "What?" she asked, opening the other eye. "I'm too full for a midnight snack...did you see how many tacos I ate?"

Rob grinned. "It's not something to eat."

Now he had her attention. She sat up a bit straighter, a

smile slowly forming. "Then what's behind your back?" she asked.

Rob pulled one arm forward and set a rectangle shaped velvet box on her lap.

"What's this?" she asked, looking over at him as he sat down next to her.

"Open it and find out," he said.

"It's not my birthday," she said, eyeing him. "And it's way too early for Christmas or Hanukkah."

"I don't need an occasion to give you a present, Hailey," he said in a low voice. His brown eyes were kind. "You deserve presents for no reason at all."

She felt warmth spread over her chest. The normally uncomfortable feeling she got around presents was replaced by sheer joy. She felt safe with Rob. She slowly opened the hinged lid of the box. Inside was a gold charm bracelet with several charms attached to it. She lifted it out.

"I know how much you liked the one Matt gave you…his was all about himself…this one is all about you…I thought of everything you loved and added it as a charm."

She began to finger the bracelet. From it hung a tiny dachshund, a stack of books, a coffee cup, a baseball mitt with a baseball, a beach umbrella, a Chinese takeout box, and a heart covered in red enamel on one side. "Rob, it's beautiful," she said, softly. "I love it. It's the best present I think I've ever gotten." She felt hot tears prick behind her eyes. It was the nicest, most beautiful, and most thoughtful gift she'd ever gotten. She knew this with certainty. And it was for no reason at all, other than he loved her. Her eyes began to sting as the tears threatened to roll.

Rob clasped the bracelet around her wrist. "Read the back of the heart," he said, his voice low.

Hailey touched the red heart and turned it to the gold side. "RES" was engraved. She gave him a confused look.

"Have I ever told you my middle name is Edward?" He smiled at her.

Her eyebrows went up when it hit her. "They're your initials!"

"I want you to have my heart, Hailey. It's yours for as long as you'll have it." His eyes held hers.

The damn burst and the tears fell. "I'll take good care of it, I promise," she said through her sobs.

Rob pulled her close to him and stroked her hair. "I love you, Hailey. You deserve everything in this life." He took her face in both hands and kissed her tears away.

Like the pressure the earth exerted to produce a diamond, the years of being friends had built up something just as treasured and beautiful between Rob and Hailey.

EPILOGUE

EXTRA INNINGS: *Additional innings needed to determine a winner if a game is tied after the regulation number of innings. Also known as bonus baseball or free baseball because paying spectators are witnessing more action than normal.*

Twenty months later...

"It's so adorable how he looks at you," Hailey said. She put her hands up to her heart. "Seriously...the cutest thing I've ever seen."

Rob smiled down at the small bundle he was holding. "It is. He's so cute."

"I wonder how Sandy will react?" Hailey asked, looking at Rob.

"I don't know," Rob replied, letting out a sigh. "I mean...I hope he doesn't get jealous, but I guess that's a risk. If he does, I hope it doesn't last long. He's got to know we still love him."

Hailey peeked over and peered into the small brown eyes. "Have you thought of a name?" She put her arm on Rob's and looked up at him. He was totally smitten already, his face soft and his lips curled into a smile.

"Uh huh. I want to name him Randy." He glanced down at Hailey.

Her brows narrowed, she looked at Rob. "Nope. No way. Not going to happen." She stepped back and folded her arms over her chest.

"Why not?" He looked over at her. His mouth pulled down into a frown.

"Because I'm not having two dogs named Randy and Sandy. That's why." She moved her hands to her hips, an incredulous expression across her face.

"But you got to name *your* dog after *your* favorite pitcher, it's only fair that I get to name *my* dog after mine." He leaned down and planted a small kiss on the head of the tiny puppy he was holding. "Isn't that right, Randy?"

"First off, they're *our* dogs. C'mon…we don't live in a divided household. Sandy loves you like you're his daddy and I plan on being mommy to this baby." She then leaned over and kissed the dog, running a finger along his forehead. "Why don't you name him Johnson then. That works." She looked at Rob.

"*Really* Hailey?"

"What?" She looked at him, eyebrows up, a questioning expression on her face."

"I'm not naming a wiener-dog Johnson," he deadpanned.

Hailey snorted. "I see what you mean."

They sat together on the bench of the shelter's puppy visiting room. They had completed adoption paperwork a few months back at the local no-kill shelter. They requested a dachshund but if after a few months there hadn't been any surrendered they would consider other smallish dogs. They had gotten a call several weeks ago that the shelter had taken in a very pregnant dachshund and if they wanted one of the puppies, sight unseen, they would need to give a non-refundable deposit. They hadn't thought twice about it. Rob and Hallie had pondered what other breed would be at play here. They were happy with any outcome and were truly delighted that the dog would be at least half dachshund. They were giddy when the shelter contacted them after momma dog gave birth to five small nuggets. A few weeks later it had been clear that her hook-up had been with another dachshund. They couldn't have been happier.

Hailey tucked a stray piece of blond hair behind her ear. "How about 'Dodger'?" She had a small smile on her face as she looked into Rob's eyes.

He responded with his own smile. "I like it. Like a Dodger Dog."

Dodger Dogs were what the hot dogs sold at Dodger Stadium were called.

Hailey nodded. "A wiener-dog named Dodger." Her grin spread across her entire face. "It's perfect."

Rob looked down at the tiny puppy whose brown eyes were looking at him. The small mouth formed in a tiny 'O.' "What do you think about that little Dodger?" He brought the dog up to his face and received some small licks in return.

A woman poked her head into the room. "I'm afraid I need to take him back to mom. It's feeding time." She smiled as Rob handed off the small bundle to her.

"When will he be ready to go home?" Hailey asked.

"About four more weeks," she replied.

Rob and Hailey made their way out of the shelter and headed to the subway station. They got off at Grand Central and began to make their way down Park Avenue to their apartment in the Murray Hill neighborhood of Manhattan. Rob's hand found Hailey's and he laced his fingers with hers. The early spring afternoon was glorious. The sky was bright blue, and the temperature was a perfect seventy degrees. The median strip down Park Avenue was lush with tulips in yellows, oranges, and pinks.

Shortly after Hailey and Sandy had moved in with Rob, she'd gotten an offer from a boutique publishing house in New York. The literary agent of one of her clients had recommended her upon hearing that they were looking for a senior editor. She'd flown out for the interview with Rob and immediately fell in love with New York. She'd never been there before, and the city captured her heart. Instantly. But roadblocks stood in the way. First and foremost was Rob. They'd just gotten together and there was no way she was going to try her hand at a long-distance relationship. The second roadblock was moving away from family, specifically Rob's family which had become Hailey's family. She would also be leaving her friends. And the third problem, although it probably would seem silly to anyone else, was that she didn't want to move away from Dodger Stadium. The thought of not spending countless days and nights watching the Boys in Blue play her favorite sport tugged at her heart. She would also miss Daisy. Daisy's father had recently remarried and his new wife, Vanessa, had taken to Daisy like a momma bear and the two had formed a close bond. Hailey would miss Daisy but felt she would be in good hands.

Slowly, and one by one, she and Rob worked through all the stumbling blocks. He'd told her there were plenty of law firms practicing sports law in Manhattan. He'd even gone so far as to reach out to a couple along with his resume. He'd quickly been offered a great position at one of the most respected firms in the industry. They offered to make him senior counsel and promised to make him a partner within two years. The issue of family and friends was harder to solve. Hailey had taken to Rob's family like a fish takes to water. She embraced their love and support. Leaving them behind would be difficult.

The issue of the Dodgers and Dodger Stadium was tricky although far less important. Hailey had come around to the idea of filling her baseball needs by attending Mets games. She was a staunch National League fan and couldn't stomach the idea of setting foot in Yankee Stadium, unless of course it was one of the times every few years that her Dodgers would be there. She and Rob had grown fond of the Mets and attended as many games as they could.

They worked out with Daisy's father and step-mom to have her visit them in New York over the summer and winter breaks, plus Hailey would see her whenever she was back in LA. She would keep in close contact for life with the girl who was now turning into a young woman.

They circled around the issue of leaving Rob's family. They could fly back to LA as often as possible and Rob's family could visit them in New York. Rob also discovered that he had a couple of cousins living in the city and vowed to become close to them. After much consideration and many conversations with his parents, brother, and grandparents, he and Hailey decided to give it a go. Everyone said that the opportunity to live in New York was not something to pass up.

Luckily Rob's house had appreciated quite a bit since he'd bought it. They used the proceeds from the sale to buy a nice two-bedroom apartment. The second bedroom being reserved for guests. It was in a pre-war building and was both charming and cozy. They'd never once regretted their decision to relocate.

Rob pulled her hand up to his mouth and lightly brushed

his lips over the back of her hand. He glanced at the ring and then looked up at her, giving her a wink. "Are you getting used to wearing it?"

Hailey looked down at the round solitaire diamond ring on her left hand. Molly had helped Rob pick it out and they'd both decided that the 2-carat unadorned simple round solitaire set in platinum suited Hailey the best. "Round like a baseball," Rob had said.

She looked up at him after touching the ring. "I'm never taking it off. Ever." She leaned up on her tiptoes and kissed him on the lips. She smiled into his chocolate brown eyes as she remembered the day just weeks earlier when he'd asked her to marry him. They'd been in LA visiting his family and Rob surprised her with tickets to a Dodger game while they were there. He told her he'd pulled some strings and was able to have her be able to throw out the first pitch at that night's game. She was over the moon excited and had practiced with him at the local park. She had been pretty sure she could get the ball to the plate. And she had...just barely. She was busy getting her picture taken with Will Smith, the Dodgers catcher and when she'd turned around Rob was down on one knee. She'd never been so shocked or so emotional in her entire life. She ugly cried her way through the whole thing and there were photos to prove it. Rob hugged her tightly, whispering in her ear that she was the only woman for him, and he would count himself lucky in this life if he could spend the rest of his days with her. The wedding was planned for the following spring in LA.

She smiled at him. "I love you Rob. I can't imagine being anywhere else in this world than right here with you by my side." Her heart swelled. She was loved. And that was everything.

AFTERWORD

Dear Reader,

Thank you for taking the time to read "Stuck on First." I hope it gave you a some laughs, made you smile, and provided a few hours of welcome distraction.

Reviews are the lifeblood of an author's life. Please take a minute to leave a review on Amazon and/or Goodreads. I cannot even begin to express my gratitude for each and every review...even if you didn't enjoy it. I read all of my reviews and try to learn from them.

I also enjoy hearing from you! Please feel free to send me an email or DM me. Contact me.

I'm currently working on the next two books in this series. The only hint I'll give at this time is that one book will feature Spencer. It's a reverse grumpy/sunshine and reverse age/gap story. The other book will feature Molly. That story is a fake marriage, enemies to lovers. Visit my website at Emilyfrenchbooks.com to sign up for my newsletter. I keep my readers updated on new works and sometimes drop a little note if anything exciting is happening in my area of the world.

Thank you for your support!
Happy Reading,
Emily

ACKNOWLEDGMENTS

When an author writes a book they often draw from bits and pieces of personal experiences. I'm no different in this area. My husband and I met on a baseball chat board and some of our personal experiences show up in this story. It was at a spring training game where my husband witnessed a woman not much different from the Georgia peach in this story who sauntered up and wanted to know "which one was Mark McGwire." It was also my husband's idea to write a romcom involving baseball since I adore the sport and it's a huge part of my life from April through November. Thank you to him for all of his support and great ideas and input. I couldn't ask for a better partner in life.

Thank you to my daughter Katy and my dear friend April. They are my best cheerleaders and sounding boards. Their support is invaluable to me. Thank you.

Emily

ABOUT THE AUTHOR

Emily French is originally from California. She is a former divorce attorney. She currently lives in North Carolina with her husband and their two dogs. When she isn't writing she can be found cooking, reading, traveling, watching baseball, and getting to know all the dogs in her neighborhood.

ALSO BY EMILY FRENCH

Made in United States
Troutdale, OR
05/09/2024

19764147R00127